GERTRUDE, GUMSHOE

and the

VardSale Villain

ROBIN MERRILL

New Creation Publishing

New Creation Publishing
Madison, Maine

Cover by Taste & See Design
Formatting by PerryElisabethDesign.com

1

Gertrude was having a bad day. She'd woken up too early and hadn't been able to fall back asleep. Her lower back was killing her, and she wasn't quite sure why. All she knew was she couldn't find a comfortable position. Sitting was almost impossible. Standing wasn't much better. To make matters worse, it was unseasonably warm for a Maine spring, and she couldn't seem to cool off.

She had opened all the windows in her trailer, and was digging through a back room full of "summer supplies," looking for her fans, when she heard a knock on her door. This surprised her—she never got company—and she stood up abruptly, causing a sharp pain to shoot down her left leg. "Ow!" she cried, though her many cats were her only potential sympathizers.

By the time she and her walker got to the door, she was out of breath and sweat dripped down her face. It had been some time since she'd heard the knock, so she flung the door open, afraid that her caller had already left.

He hadn't.

"Well hi there, Andy! What are you doing here?"

Andy gave her a half-smile. "I'm surprised you remember me. It's been a while."

"That it has. Do you still work down at the gentleman's club?"

"Well, you're the only one who calls it that, but yes, I'm still at Private Eyes." He stopped talking and stared at her as if waiting for her to say something.

After a long pause that would have felt awkward to most people, but not so much to Gertrude, she asked, "So what brings you to my neck of the woods?"

Andy looked down, as if embarrassed about something.

"What's wrong, Andy? Cat got your tongue? Around here, that's possible." She laughed at her joke. He did not. *Some people just have no sense of humor.*

"Could I come in?"

Gertrude took a step back. "I s'pose so, but it's hotter than a hoochie coochie in here."

Andy chuckled, but it sounded forced. He stepped inside, and his eyes grew wide as he looked around her home. "Wow, you sure do have a lot of ... stuff."

Gertrude's chest grew tight with defensiveness. "I'm a collector. Wouldn't be a very good collector if I didn't collect things. Now what can I do for you?"

Andy started to shut the door behind him.

"Leave it open. It's a lot cooler out there."

"Won't your cats get out?" As he spoke the words, Lightning zipped through the doorway.

"Yes, but that's all right. My neighbors love cats." *At least, none of them have ever complained. That I know of.*

"Anyway," Andy continued, his eyes scanning the room again as if he just couldn't believe what he was seeing, "are you still doing that private investigating thing?"

Gertrude's heart leapt. "Why, yes I am!"

Andy looked at her. His eyes were steady, unemotional. "How much do you charge?"

Gertrude frowned. She had no idea how much she charged. No one had ever paid her for her services. "Twelve dollars an hour?" she guessed.

Andy nodded and looked around again. "Do you think maybe you could work for a few hours, see what you could find out for me? I don't have much money, but I really need some help."

"Sure!" Gertrude trembled with excitement. This would be her very first paying client. Her first *willing* client. "What's the case?"

"My girlfriend is missing."

"Oh," Gertrude said, feeling a little guilty for being excited about such a pickle. But only a little. "Have you gone to the police?"

Andy looked disgusted at the idea. "Aren't they kind of your competition? Why do you want me to go to them?"

"Because if your girlfriend is in danger, we want all hands on deck, right? The cops aren't my competition. It's more like I work alongside them." This was sort of true.

Andy grimaced. "Yes, I told them, and they don't care. Or they don't believe me. I don't know. She's only been missing for a day, and they seem to think she's not really missing. They acted like I've been dumped and just don't know it yet."

"Have you?"

"Have I what?"

"Been dumped?"

"No! Look, I really love Samantha. And she loves me. This isn't just some fling. We're going to get married. This is unlike any other relationship I've ever had. It's for real, and she wouldn't just up and leave me. Something is really wrong. I can feel it."

"All right, Andy. I was just asking. How long has she been missing?"

"She went to work yesterday. I talked to her coworker—"

"Where does she work?"

"Hospital. She's a CNA."

"Hang on," Gertrude said. "Let me get some note-taking implements." She hobbled into the kitchen.

"You OK?"

"Yep, just got a little ache in my upper tuchus, is all." She rummaged through a drawer and came up with a pad of paper and a pen. She returned to find him staring at her. "What?"

"Nothing. Just wondering if I've lost my mind asking you for help. You're not exactly a typical private investigator."

"Nothing good about typical, no there ain't. Besides, I'm the only one in town. Now, what's your girlfriend's last name?"

"Actually, no, you're not the only one in town."

Gertrude's head snapped up. "What?"

"Colby Rodin."

"Who in tarnation is Colby Rodin?"

"He's a PI. Got an office downtown. Been there for years."

"Well, I've never heard of him. So he must not be anything to write home about. Besides, you're *here*, aren't you?"

"He charges fifty dollars an hour and a two hundred dollar retainer."

"I see." Gertrude wished she'd given more thought to her hourly rate. "Well anyway, you're here now, so let's get to work. Her name is Samantha what?"

"Cooper."

"All right," Gertrude said, writing that down, "and she's a CNA at the hospital?"

"Yes."

"And she went to work yesterday?"

"Yes."

"What were her hours?"

"Seven to six."

"Wowsa, that's a long shift."

"Yeah, but she only works four days a week, so she likes it. Today was the first day of her three days off, and we were supposed to go for a hike ..." Andy's voice trailed off.

The sadness in it made Gertrude acutely uncomfortable.

"Pretty muddy for a hike," Gertrude commented.

"Yeah. Samantha is outdoorsy. And she can talk me into anything." He sounded even sadder.

"All right, so did she work her full shift?"

"Yes, I talked to a girl who works with her, and she said that Sam left work at the normal time, and was in a good mood and everything."

"What time did she leave exactly?"

"Six."

Gertrude wrote that down. "And do you know if anyone has seen her since?"

"I don't think so. She never went home last night—"

"*Went* home? You two don't cohabitate?"

"No. She wanted to wait till we were married."

Gertrude raised an eyebrow. "Old-fashioned girl, eh?"

"As I was saying, her roommate, Akayla, said she hasn't come back to her apartment.

She hasn't heard from her either. But there is this ..." He pulled his cell out of his back pocket. "Sam had an appointment with someone named Patsy at six-thirty. I don't know what this is, or who Patsy is, but it just appeared on our calendar yesterday."

"*Our* calendar?" Gertrude asked, confused.

"Yeah, we share a Google calendar. So she added this sometime yesterday, but I don't know when." He held the phone out to her.

She didn't take it. She wasn't sure why he wanted her to. "And does it say where the appointment was?"

"No. It just says 'Patsy,' which you could see for yourself if you would just take the phone."

Gertrude ignored his outstretched phone and wrote, "Andy can be rude," on her notepad.

Finally, he gave up and put the phone back in his pocket.

"Did you tell the cops about Patsy?"

"They didn't let me get that far."

"All right, what else do we know?" Gertrude asked.

"That's it."

"That's it?"

"Yep. She's missing. Her car's missing. I can't find anyone who has seen her. And I don't know who Patsy is. You now know everything I know."

"OK, can you take me to her apartment?"

"Uh ... sure. You want me to drive you?"

"Yes. I need a ride."

"You don't have a car?"

"I do not."

"What kind of a private investigator has no car?"

2

Akayla answered the door seconds after Andy knocked, and then looked annoyed when she saw that it was him.

Gertrude stepped forward. "I'm Gertrude. When was the last time you saw Samantha?"

"Why?" Akayla said, alarmed. "Did something happen?"

"Yes, something happened," Andy snapped. "That's what I've been trying to tell you!"

Akayla ignored him and looked at Gertrude. "What happened?"

"That's what we're trying to figure out. When was the last time you saw her?"

"Yesterday morning. When she left for work."

"Can we come in and look around?" Gertrude asked, stepping inside before Akayla could protest.

Akayla gave Andy a questioning look, to which he said, "She's a private investigator. Sort of."

"Andy, I thought the cops said there was nothing to worry about," Akayla said.

"They did, but they don't know Sam. She wouldn't just vanish unless something is wrong. Maybe if you call them, they'll take the whole thing seriously."

She nodded. "OK. I'll call them right now." She headed toward the kitchen.

Gertrude called after her, "Do you know anyone named Patsy?"

She located her phone on the cluttered kitchen table. "No," she said, coming back toward them. "Andy already asked me that. Why, who's Patsy?"

"That's what we're trying to figure out," Gertrude said. "But if the cops will let you, you might want to mention that Samantha had an appointment with a person named Patsy last night."

"OK," Akayla said, and dialed the phone.

"Also, don't mention to the cops that I'm here," Gertrude added.

This imperative appeared to vex Akayla. "Why?"

"They don't like me." Gertrude looked at Andy. "Take me to Samantha's bedroom."

He led the way down a narrow hallway and then stopped at a door to his left. He gingerly opened it as if afraid something was going to jump out at him. As the door slowly swung open, he just stood there, looking into the bedroom.

"Well?" Gertrude prodded. "Either go in or get out of my way!"

He stepped aside. "Sorry. I just … I've never been in her bedroom. Just feels wrong. Like I'm invading her privacy."

"No problem," Gertrude said, pushing past him. "I'll invade it."

The room was a mess. The bed was unmade. There were piles of clothing on the floor, and more heaped on her dresser. A jewelry armoire stood open, with dozens of necklaces hanging from the hooks. *She must not have a cat*, Gertrude thought. Samantha's mirror was decorated with pictures of her and Andy, most of them taken outside. "She's a looker," Gertrude remarked.

"I know," Andy said dolefully.

Gertrude plucked one of the photos from the mirror, a close-up of the two of them, smiling, the wind blowing their hair back. "Can I keep this one for a while?"

"Sure."

She heard fear in his voice, so she added, "Just till we find her, Andy. I'll give it back to her then."

Andy nodded.

To avoid any more interaction with Andy's emotions, Gertrude began rifling through Samantha's drawers. As she was doing this, Akayla appeared in the doorway. "The cops took the information down. Said they'd start looking for her and her car."

"Wow, you had a lot more pull than I did," Andy said.

Akayla gave him a look that said, *Of course I did.* Then she looked at Gertrude. "Are you sure you need to go through her drawers?"

"Just looking for anything out of the ordinary," Gertrude muttered. What she wanted to say was, "Don't question my methods. I'm the professional here."

"Why don't the cops like you?" Akayla asked.

"Long story," Gertrude said, as she slid her hands along the bottom of the drawers, searching for hidden clues. Finding none, she stood up straight, her back cracking. "Did you tell them about Patsy?"

"Yep," Akayla said. "Should I help you look?"

"Sure," Gertrude said. "She sure does have a lot of clothes."

"It's kind of an addiction of hers. Clothes and jewelry. Purses and scarves. She hated that she had to wear scrubs to work. But she got all this stuff used, so it's an inexpensive addiction."

Andy let out a soft moan. Gertrude looked up at him. He was white as a sheet. She didn't know if she'd ever seen anyone look so sad and so scared.

"Why don't you go sit down for a spell, Andy? We've got this," Gertrude said.

Without a word, Andy disappeared down the hallway.

Akayla moved the blankets on the bed around, revealing a laptop. She flipped it open and sat down on the bed. "I'm going to look on her Facebook page. See if there's a Patsy."

"Oh, good idea," Gertrude said. "Facebook has helped me solve every mystery so far."

Akayla looked unconvinced. Her fingers skittered across the keyboard.

"Wowsa! You type with both hands! With all fingers too!"

Akayla, either not hearing this odd compliment or choosing to ignore it, said, "Aw, crap!"

"What?" Gertrude said, leaning in to peer at the screen.

"She's got her privacy settings all jacked up. I can't even see her friends list."

"Why would she do that?" Gertrude asked. "She got something to hide?"

"No!" Akayla said defensively. "She's an attractive woman in an ugly world. And she's smart. I should've guessed she'd be keeping her account pretty private. She doesn't spend much time on Facebook anyway."

Gertrude sat beside Akayla on the bed. Akayla scooted several inches away from her. "Where does Sam spend her time?" Gertrude asked.

"At work. Or outside."

"No, I mean on the computer. Can you tell what internet places she's visited lately? She must have been doing something. She had the computer in her bed."

"Good point. Let me check her history." Akayla tapped some keys and then muttered as she read, "Natural Health News, Netflix, Best Hiking Trails in Maine, and *VardSale*? What the heck is VardSale?"

"How should I know? Click on it."

"I just did."

The two women sat, uncomfortably close to each other, staring at the laptop screen.

Finally, something loaded. "Welcome to VardSale, your virtual yard sale experience!" Akayla read aloud.

"Wowsa!" Gertrude said. "This looks like fun!"

"Maybe," Akayla said, her brow furrowed, "but I'm not really sure why we need a virtual yard sale experience when we already have Craigslist and Uncle Henry's."

"I *love* Uncle Henry's," Gertrude cooed. "Got many of my treasures that way. And a few of my cats. But that's just a book. It's not on the computer."

Akayla looked at her as if she were stupid. "Uncle Henry's is absolutely a website. Where you been?"

"Oh. I still get mine in the mail. Excuuuuse me!"

"It looks like she's got some notifications," Akayla said, and clicked on a bell icon. "Looks like she's been trying to buy all sorts of stuff."

"Click on the little envelope." Gertrude pointed a stubby finger at the screen.

"That's her messages. She doesn't have any new ones, or it would tell us."

"Just do it."

Akayla clicked.

They both gasped.

Samantha had been talking to someone named Patsy Pelotte. Silently, both women read the conversation. And it was lengthy. Patsy seemed to be far more motivated to engage in small talk than to sell anything. She wrote a lot about the weather, her favorite television shows, and even asked questions about Samantha's boyfriend, which Samantha had deftly dodged.

Smart girl.

Samantha had agreed to meet Patsy behind the New Balance factory, when she got out of work at six-thirty. She was going to give Patsy three dollars for a pair of Nike sneakers.

"Scandalous!" Gertrude remarked.

"What?"

"Selling Nikes at a New Balance factory."

"We should call the cops, tell them to go look there for her car," Akayla said, ignoring Gertrude's joke.

"You do that. First, can you click on Patsy? Maybe see a profile or something? I think it's a little odd that she would get out of work at six-thirty, when the factory lets out at three."

"Maybe she works security or something," Akayla offered. She clicked on Patsy's name and a new page loaded. Then Akayla said a bad word.

The screen read, "This user account has been removed."

"Oh succotash!" Gertrude exclaimed.

"I'm calling the cops."

"You do that," Gertrude said, and got up to go fill Andy in.

3

Much to Gertrude's dismay, the sheriff's department beat Andy, Akayla, and her to the New Balance factory parking lot. Samantha's blue Corolla was surrounded by deputies. One was digging in the trunk. One was sitting in the driver's seat. Deputy Hale, Gertrude's least favorite law enforcement professional, was standing off to the side, hands on his hips, apparently supervising.

As the motley threesome climbed out of Andy's car, Deputy Hale winced at the sight of Gertrude. "What are you doing here?" he asked.

"Samantha is a friend of mine," Gertrude said.

"Of course she is. Well, there's nothing to see here. This is a crime scene—"

"Crime scene?" Andy cried, taking a step toward the car. "Why, what did you find?"

"Take it easy, sir," Hale said, using a professional voice Gertrude hadn't heard him use before. He stepped between Andy and the Toyota. "We haven't found anything. But we are considering this a missing person case now. No reason to worry yet, but we are now actively looking for her. You're the boyfriend?"

Andy swallowed hard, and nodded.

"Can you come down to the office, answer a few questions?"

Andy glared at Hale. "I was at the office this morning, and no one could be bothered to ask me any questions."

"I understand your frustration, sir. We're listening now. Can you come to the office?"

"It's all right, Andy," Gertrude said. "Go answer their questions. It might help. Tell them about VardSale." She lowered her voice so only Andy could hear. "In the meantime, I'll keep investigating."

Andy nodded, appeared to be fighting back tears, and said to Hale, "OK, I'll meet you there."

"Wait," Akayla said. "We rode with you. You can't just leave us here, stranded at the New Balance factory on the hottest day of the year!"

"What is your name?" Hale asked.

"Akayla Malone."

"And what's your relationship to Samantha Cooper?"

"I'm her roommate. I'm the one who told you where the car was."

"OK, well, we're going to have to ask you a few questions too. Can you come with Andy to the office?"

Akayla groaned and folded her arms across her chest.

"What are you going to do for a ride?" Andy asked Gertrude.

"Don't you worry your handsome little head. I'll just call Norm."

Norman was one of the drivers of the CAP bus (a van provided by Community Action Program). Gertrude didn't know if he was on duty at the moment, but she hoped. She dialed the familiar number to ask for a ride, and sure enough, it was Norman who pulled into the parking lot.

"That's a lot of blue lights," Norman said as Gertrude heaved herself into the van. "What have you got yourself mixed up in now, Gertrude?"

She pulled her walker into the van behind her and then slammed the door. "Norm, I'm happy to share with you that I officially have my first paying client."

Norman glanced at her in the rearview. "Has he actually paid you anything yet?"

"Norm! Don't be nasty. His girlfriend's missing."

"Missing? Wow, so it's like a real case?" Norman pulled out onto Route 201.

"Of course it's a real case. Real as crunchy peanut butter. And yes, she's missing. Hasn't been seen since she left work yesterday at six. She had the name Patsy on her fancy

26

calendar app for six-thirty. Do you know anyone named Patsy?"

Norman appeared to be thinking it over. "I don't think so. Nothing comes to mind except Patsy Cline."

"Well, I doubt ole Patsy is snatching young women off the street. That's just *Crazy*." She laughed at her joke.

Norman either didn't get the reference or just didn't think it was funny.

"Norm, you ever heard of VardSale?"

Norman chuckled. "Yeah. My daughter-in-law is kind of obsessed with it. Apparently you can buy and sell just about anything on there. She claims to have made a lot of money selling 'décor.' I don't know what décor is, or how she makes so much of it, but apparently, it sells like hotcakes."

"Hmm … that's fascinating, Norm. Could you ask her for me if she's ever dealt with anyone named Patsy?"

"Sure. You want me to do it right now?"

"You mean call her?"

"Well, she's not in the van, so yes, I would use a telephone. But I'll have to pull over. It's against the rules to drive and use the phone at the same time. You in a hurry?"

"Nah. Go for it."

Norman pulled the CAP bus into the dollar store parking lot. Gertrude had the urge to jump out and go shop, but she didn't want to miss the conversation.

"Hey, Melody, it's Norm ... Yeah, I'm good, thanks ... No, it's much better now. Hey, I've got a friend here who wanted me to ask you if you've ever dealt with anyone on VardSale named Patsy—"

"Put it on speaker phone," Gertrude said.

"Hey, hang on, Melody, I'm going to put you on speaker." He pressed a button. "OK, so as I was saying. You know anyone from VardSale named Patsy?"

"Pelotte," Gertrude said. "Tell her *Pelotte*."

"Patsy Pelotte," Norman repeated.

"No, I don't think so. I've dealt with so many women, though. Maybe if I could see a picture?"

Gertrude shook her head at Norman. "Her profile's been deleted. If she's the kidnapper, she probably wouldn't have posted a photo anyway—"

"Kidnapper?" Melody practically shrieked. "What's going on?"

Norman gave Gertrude a disappointed look. "No, no, Melody, don't worry. My friend here has a flare for the dramatic. We don't know if anyone has been kidnapped. We're just looking for someone."

"OK, well don't expect VardSale to help. I called them once because I accidentally deleted a phone number that I needed for a buyer, and they wouldn't help me at all. Went on and on about respecting their users' privacy. Not that they would know anything about 'Patsy' anyway, if that's even her real name. Anyone can make an account in like two seconds. The best they could probably find is an IP address, and I doubt they'd give it to you."

"OK, well, thanks, Melody. I've got to get back on the road. But you be extra careful with these VardSale deals, OK? Make sure you always meet in a well-lit area, with lots of people around. You hear me?"

"You bet, Pops. And if you know anyone who needs décor—"

"I know, I know, send them to you. Bye bye now." Norman hung up the phone. "Sorry, that wasn't much help."

Gertrude scrunched up her face. "What in tarnation is an IP address?"

4

Norman started to slow the van down in front of Gertrude's trailer.

"Actually, Norm, can you take me two doors down? To Calvin's place?"

Norman gave her a suggestive look she didn't care for. "You been consortin' with Old Man Crow?"

"Don't be ridiculous. I just need his computer. And his air conditioning."

"OK then. Here you go."

"Thanks, Norm."

Gertrude climbed the few steps to Calvin's door and then pounded on it.

"I'm coming, I'm coming, hold your horses," Calvin hollered, and then ripped the door open.

"Ah," Gertrude exclaimed, stepping inside. "That cold air feels good."

"Don't you have an air conditioner, Gert? This is the twenty-first century."

"I have several air conditioners. But none of them are working right now." Gertrude plopped onto the sofa and put one foot on Calvin's coffee table.

"Have a seat," Calvin said to Gertrude.

"Thanks, but I already did," Gertrude said, honestly confused. "So, we've got a case."

"A-yuh," Calvin said doubtfully.

"No, a real one. As in someone is paying me. You remember Andy, the janitor from the strip club?"

"The one you claimed was from Cambodia?"

Gertrude frowned. "I don't remember saying that. But we've only met one strip club janitor. Anyway, he has hired me to find his missing girlfriend."

Calvin smoothed out his pants and sat down. "She's really missing?"

"Yes. Really. And we need your computer."

Calvin heaved a great sigh. "Here we go again. Gertrude, why don't you get your own computer?"

"I might have to, you keep giving me so much grief about using yours."

Calvin stood back up and crossed the room to his computer desk. He jiggled the mouse, bringing the screen to life. "What do you need?"

"I think we need to create a VardSale account."

"*VardSale*? What's that?"

"Near as we can tell, it's a buy and sell website, like Uncle Henry's, only online," Gertrude explained.

"Uncle Henry's *is* online," Calvin said.

"So I've heard. Anyway. Just type it in—V-A-R-D-S-A-L-E," she spelled.

"OK," he said. "I'm here. Now why am I here?"

Gertrude got up and hobbled toward him. "The last thing we know about Samantha's—

she's the missing girl—schedule is that she was supposed to meet someone named Patsy Pelotte from this website, to buy a pair of sneakers. Her car is still at the meeting place, but she isn't. She hasn't been seen since, that we know of." She winced and shifted her weight to the other foot.

"You all right?" Calvin asked.

"Yep. Just a little back pain is all."

"You want some ibuprofen?" he offered.

"Nah, don't need any of that stuff fogging up my mind."

"Oh yeah." Calvin laughed. "Your mind is sharp as a tack."

"All right," Gertrude said, pointing her chin at the screen and ignoring his jab, "right there it says 'Join now.' Click it."

"My, my, aren't we bossy today?" he said, and clicked the button.

"Either type my name into the box, or get up so I can," Gertrude said.

Calvin looked up at her, but this means he only looked up a few inches, as she was barely taller than him when he was seated.

"Are you sure you want to use your real name? What's the plan here?"

"Not sure. I think best on the fly—"

Calvin snorted.

"What?" Gertrude asked defensively.

"You *think* you think best on the fly, because you don't ever try to think pre-flight."

Gertrude frowned. "That didn't make any sense, Calvin. Now, as I was saying, I don't really have a plan yet. But you're right. Better not use my name. Old Patsy, or whoever she is, might recognize my name as the local gumshoe."

Calvin laughed again. "Good point. OK, what's your alias then?"

"Oooo, an alias. Like a code name! I've always wanted to need a code name." She thought for a minute. "And I've always wanted to be named Hazel."

"Hazel. Of course. How youthful."

"Really? You think Hazel's youthful?" Gertrude was delighted.

Calvin shook his head. "Hazel what?"

"Hazel Green?"

Calvin looked up at her. "Don't you think that sounds a little fake?"

"I know!" Gertrude snickered. "Hazel Hale!"

Calvin shook his head. "Nope. She might actually recognize that name. We don't want her to think you're a cop's grandmother."

"I'm not old enough to be Hale's grandmother! Are you bonkers?"

Calvin looked at her thoughtfully. "Gertrude, I know this is impolite to ask, but ..." He hesitated.

"But what?"

"Well, one can't help but wonder, just *how old are you*?"

Gertrude scowled.

"I mean, it is just a little unusual. Because you don't *look* very old, but you act ..." He hesitated again.

"I act what?"

"You know what? Never mind. Where were we?" He looked at the computer. "Ah yes, your new last name."

Gertrude was still scowling. "You pick. Make it youthful so it will match Hazel."

Calvin didn't say anything. He just typed Hazel Walker into the field. Then it asked for her zip code. He entered it. Two green buttons appeared. Sell or shop. Calvin looked up at her. "Which one?"

Gertrude didn't even hesitate. "Shop." Calvin clicked the button, and the page filled with secondhand goodies. Gertrude scanned the wares. "How do you show you want to buy something?"

Calvin scrolled down. "There's a button below each item." He pointed at one. It said, "Set up a meet."

"All right then. Let's set up some meets. Then we'll ask people if they know anyone named Patsy."

Calvin looked impressed. "That's actually a pretty good idea, Gert."

"I know."

"So what do you want to buy?"

"Go down again," Gertrude said. He scrolled. Then she said, "There!" so loudly he jumped in his chair.

"Easy, Gert. You're right in my ear, you know. Now, which one of these pieces of rubbish has you all shook up?"

"There," she said, "that cast iron cat doorstop!"

Calvin chuckled. "Of course. Gertrude, that hunk of junk is twenty bucks. Don't you want to find something cheaper?"

"No, really. I've been looking for another one of those. Besides, I can dicker. Click on it, quick, before someone else does."

"I doubt there's going to be a mad rush." Calvin clicked. It opened up a message box. He looked at Gertrude. "Now what?"

She scowled. "Not sure. Now I guess I send a message to the buyer? Type, 'Hi, I'm Gertrude.'"

"You mean Hazel? And I don't think we need to chitchat. The button said 'Set up a meet,' so let's offer a meeting place and time."

"All right, then. How about my trailer ..." Gertrude looked around for a clock. "What time is it?"

"Time's right there on the screen, Gertrude," Calvin said, pointing to the bottom corner of the monitor. It read four o'clock.

"No wonder I'm hungry. How about four-thirty?"

"I think we need to give her more of a warning than that, Gert. Not everyone is just sitting around in their trailer waiting for something to happen."

"But I'm going to give her some cold, hard cash! That should get her up and moving! How about five o'clock then?"

Calvin sighed. "All right, we can offer that. But I don't think we should say your trailer. Let's meet somewhere public, somewhere neutral."

"Does that mean you're going to give me a ride?"

"Have you acquired a car since I've last seen you?"

"No."

"Well, then, I guess I'll give you a ride. Otherwise, you'll never leave my trailer."

5

Surprisingly, the cast iron cat doorstop owner, whose name was Carol, agreed to meet Calvin and Gertrude in the McDonald's parking lot at five.

"Hi, I'm Ger—"

Calvin elbowed her in the ribs.

"Ow!" she exclaimed. "Ahem. I'm Hazel."

"Hi, Hazel. Here's your cat." She handed the iron doorstop through her driver's side window. Gertrude took it and almost dropped it. "Wowsa! That's a heavy son of a gun. Would you take ten?"

Carol looked horrified. "No, I won't take ten! When you set up a VardSale meet, you agree to the price. You want to haggle, you do it online, not once I've driven all the way into Mattawooptock!"

"All right, all right, I'll give you twenty. Calvin, give her twenty bucks."

Calvin looked annoyed, but not necessarily surprised, as he pulled out his wallet.

"I'm sorry, Carol, I'm new to this VardSale thing."

"That's all right," Carol said, although it was clear that it wasn't.

"Are you?" Gertrude asked.

"Am I what?"

"New to VardSale?"

"No, I'm not new. I've been doing this for months now."

"Oh. Do you make any money at it?"

Carol hesitated. "A little. Why?"

"Oh, I was just thinking about selling some stuff of my own." She handed the cat to Calvin. "Take this thing, would you? It hurts my back just to hold it. Thing must weigh fifty pounds."

Calvin was obviously miffed, but he took the cat and put it in the trunk.

"All right then. You have a nice day," Carol said.

"Wait!" Gertrude cried.

"What?" Carol asked, startled.

"Have you ever dealt with anyone named Patsy Pelotte?"

"No, why?"

"Just wondering. Have you ever dealt with anyone suspicious, anyone who made you feel a little, well, *uncomfortable*?"

"You mean other than you? No."

"Well, that was rude!" Gertrude said, appalled.

Calvin returned to her side then and gave her a look that said, "Calm down!"

Gertrude tried to ignore him. "Have you seen anything out of the ordinary?" she asked Carol. "Anything at all?"

"Actually, now that you mention it," Carol said reluctantly, "something unusual did happen the other day. I was supposed to meet a woman named Martha—"

"Martha who?" Gertrude interrupted.

Carol thought. "Martha … Giles. Anyway, I was running late, and she texted me from the parking lot, said she was there, but when I got there, she was gone. And her car was just sitting there. That was pretty weird."

"And you didn't tell anyone?"

"Who am I going to tell? I didn't know where she was. I don't even know her. I just figured she gave up on me."

And left her car? What are the chances of that? "All right then. Where was her car?"

"At the Catholic church."

"Was there anyone else around?" Gertrude asked.

"No. It's a popular place for VardSalers to meet. Nice big parking lot, right off the main drag, but no, when I got there, there was no one else around."

"All right, then. Look, Carol, I know we got off to a rough start, but can I give you my business card? In case you think of anything else you can tell me?"

Calvin elbowed Gertrude in the ribs again.

"Ow!" she exclaimed, and reached into her walker pouch. Then she held out the card. Carol reached out and took it.

"Gertrude, Gumshoe?" she read, and then looked up at Gertrude, an eyebrow raised.

"That's right," Gertrude said.

"I thought your name was Hazel."

6

As soon as they were back in Calvin's car,
Gertrude fished out her Android.

"You calling Hale?" Calvin guessed.

"Don't you think I should?"

"I suppose."

"Somerset Sheriff's Department," a tired-
sounding woman answered.

"This is Gertrude. I need to speak to Deputy
Hale."

"Hold, please."

"I'm on hold," Gertrude whispered to Calvin.

"Congratulations," Calvin said.

"Hale here."

"Hi, Hale. This is Gertrude. So, I was just talking to someone from VardSale. Her name is Carol, and I met her at McDonald's to buy a cast iron cat. I offered her ten for it, but—"

"Gertrude, I'm busy. Do you have a point?"

"As a matter of fact I do, and I would've gotten to it by now if you hadn't interrupted." She took a long, deep breath before continuing, "So, as Andy probably told you by now, Samantha was supposed to meet someone from VardSale, someone named Patsy Pelotte. Well, I just met someone *else* from VardSale, and she was supposed to meet someone named Martha Giles in the Catholic church parking lot, but when she got there, Martha wasn't there. Just her car was there. Same M.O. as our case."

Hale snorted. "Same M.O.?"

"What? I've been watching *Hawaii Five-0*. I just can't get enough of Danno. You should watch it. You could learn a lot from him. Anyway, you might want to check it out. The lead, I mean, not *Hawaii Five-0*. See if you can find Martha Giles."

"OK, Gertrude. We'll do that."

"Really?"

"Yes, really." Hale paused. "Why are you being so forthcoming with your information, Gertrude?"

"What's that supposed to be mean?"

"Well, usually you just go tearing off on your own and don't tell me anything."

Blood rushed to Gertrude's head. "Hale, I'll have you know, I have tried to tell you *every*thing *every* time. It's not my fault this is the first time you've listened to me. Good day!"

Calvin laughed. "Did you just hang up on the police?"

"Yes. And it felt good."

"So you want me to take you home, or are we going back to my computer?"

"You can drop me off at home. I've got to feed my cats and take care of my new doorstop. Then I'll walk over and we can do some more shopping."

"Fine. But can you pick out some stuff *you* can pay for this time?"

"Oh, sure. And I'll pay you back for that. I just really thought I could get her down to ten dollars, so that's all I brought."

"Guess we should also read the VardSale rules too. Maybe dickering isn't the only no-no," Calvin said.

"Maybe. You think it says anything about kidnapping in there?"

"I doubt it. They probably leave that one up to common sense. Though, it might warn people against meeting alone in dark alleys. You really think this other woman was kidnapped?"

"I don't know, but something hinky is going on."

True to her word, Gertrude deposited her cat doorstop (with her four others) and then fed her living, breathing cats, taking time to greet each one by name. Lastly, she grabbed a quick bite herself, and then headed back down the street to Calvin's trailer.

He was already logged onto VardSale when she got there.

"You haven't committed me to anything else, have you?" she asked.

"Oh, right. 'Cause you're such a discriminating consumer. Heaven forbid *I* should pick something out."

"What *have* you found?"

"Lots of baby clothes. Some broken toys. Take a look for yourself," he said, standing up and stretching.

"Really? You're going to let me touch your computer?"

"I guess so, but don't make me analyze my decision, or I may change my mind. You shop. I'm going to watch *Gunsmoke*." He sat down in his armchair and reclined.

Gertrude sat down in his chair. "This is fancy!" she exclaimed.

"What?"

"Your chair. It has wheels," she said, looking down at them.

"You've never seen an office chair before?"

"And it spins!" she exclaimed. She spun herself all the way around. "Wheee!"

"Gertrude, stop it. Either get to work or go home."

"Fine," she said, grabbing the edge of the desk and stopping herself mid-spin. "Haven't you seen all the *Gunsmoke* episodes by now?"

"Haven't you seen all the *Murder, She Wrote*s?"

"That's different. I'm *studying* on how to be a good gumshoe. You're not studying on how to be a good cowboy."

"Maybe I am. Or maybe I just like to look at Miss Kitty. Or maybe there are so many episodes of *Gunsmoke*, by the time I get through them all, I've forgotten how the first ones ended. And maybe you should just do your business and let me watch my show."

"Fine, fine. No need to get all huffy about it, *Marshall*." She scrolled down the screen. "Ooo," she cooed. She clicked on the "Set up a meet" button and then started to type her message.

"You type like a chicken."

"What?"

"Peck, peck, peck."

"Can you drive me to McDonald's tomorrow at ten?"

"Sure, what are we buying?"

"A bathmat."

Calvin looked at her, frowning. "Gertrude, that's gross."

"No, it's brand-new. She only wants fifty cents for it."

"Fine. Set it up. But choose your suspects wisely. I'm not spending all day in the McDonald's parking lot."

Over the course of two *Gunsmoke* episodes, Gertrude had offered to buy fourteen different things, and three women had responded: she was going to buy a pencil sharpener from Penny, a snow globe from Jen, and a dress from Dolly.

"You've got to be kidding me," Calvin said when he looked at the list. "A snow globe?"

"Yeah, you're probably right. I don't really need another one, but I couldn't really find anything else I wanted."

"So you picked a snow globe?"

"I picked something that cost only fifty cents. You go look for something more exciting! I've been scrolling through bibs and onesies for the past two hours!"

Calvin rubbed his head. "I can't believe people go to all this trouble to make fifty cents. Why not just throw the snow globe away? Then you don't have to invest an hour of your life trying to get rid of it."

"Throw it away?" Gertrude was horrified.

"Yes, throw it away! All this time photographing things and uploading things. Then you've got to communicate with people and then actually meet them somewhere? So you've got to get in your car and drive somewhere? And then they're late, of course, because everyone is always late in this day and age. And then, finally, after all of that, what do you have to show for it? Fifty cents."

"But the other person has a snow globe."

Calvin was appalled. "Gertrude, you can go buy a new, sanitary snow globe at Walmart! And do you really think that's why this woman is selling a snow globe? So that *you* can get one? Don't be ridiculous."

"I'm not ridiculous, Calvin. I just happen to believe in not being wasteful."

Calvin shuddered. "Fine. I give up. What happened to the bathmat?"

"She never answered me."

"Well, thank God for small favors. OK, Gertrude, I need to go to bed. You want me to walk you home?"

Gertrude stared at him, speechless. Her stomach did a flip, and her palms began to sweat, despite the air conditioning.

Calvin must have noticed her discomfort, because he hastily added, "I'm not trying to get fresh or anything. I just … if there's a kidnapper out there, I want you to be safe."

"I … thank you … I'll be all right. I've got my pepper spray in my walker pouch."

Calvin laughed. "Really?"

"Really."

"OK, well, you holler if you see anything suspicious."

"You sure you're going to hear me over all that gunfire?"

"You should get going then, before the commercials are over. I turn the TV back up when my show comes back on."

7

The next morning, Gertrude woke to her cell ringing. It was Andy.

"You were right," he said, which were three of Gertrude's very favorite words. "Hale said Martha Giles is missing too."

"And no one reported it?"

"Apparently she's an older woman, lives alone. No family to notice her missing. Also, he can't find records of anyone named Patsy Pelotte. No one named Patsy works at New Balance, either."

"I see," Gertrude said, sitting up and rubbing her eyes with her free hand. The sunlight was bright through her window. She had overslept. "Oh, fiddlesticks!"

"What?"

"Oh, nothing to worry about. I'm just running a bit behind. Got to get going. I'm meeting with people from VardSale, to question them."

"How much are we up to now?"

"How much what?"

"Money?"

I have no idea, haven't been counting. "Three hours."

Andy was silent.

"It's all right, Andy. I want to find Samantha. I'll do what I can, and you pay me what you can, when you can. I'm not worried about the money."

"OK, thanks, Gertrude. I really appreciate it."

"No problem. You keep in touch. I am grateful for you being my go-between with Hale. I really don't like talking to that man. He's a meanieface."

Gertrude hung up the phone, fed the cats, hurriedly got ready, and then tried to look casual as she strode over to Calvin's house.

"Was starting to think you'd overslept," Calvin said when he opened the door.

"Me? Never! I get up with the roosters!" She stifled a yawn.

"OK, well, let's go, Foghorn."

Gertrude chortled. "If I'm Foghorn, does that make you Miss Prissy?"

Calvin opened the rear door of the Cadillac so that Gertrude could stow her walker inside. Then they both climbed into the front.

"Wowsa, it's already warm out," Gertrude said. "Going to be another scorcher, I think."

Calvin didn't say anything, but he did turn up the air conditioner.

As Calvin drove, Gertrude filled him in on what Andy had told her about the missing Martha Giles.

"It's kind of weird, isn't it?" Calvin remarked.

"What?"

"Having an actual client? Someone who actually *wants* our help?"

"You could get used to this, couldn't you?" Gertrude said.

Calvin seemed to come back to himself. "I didn't say that. I'm liable to get myself killed before that happens. You hungry?"

"I could eat."

Calvin took Gertrude through the drive through. They each got a sausage biscuit and a coffee. He paid, of course. Then they parked where Penny had told them to.

"Why are we parked by the dumpster?" he complained.

"I dunno. Guess so we'll be out of the way."

"Well this is a stinky, unsanitary place to hang out."

"Stop grumbling, you old grump."

"What are we buying from this one again?" Calvin asked.

Gertrude took another bite of her biscuit and then said through a full mouth, "Pencil sharpener."

"Who the heck sells a pencil sharpener? Aren't they like ten cents new?"

Gertrude swallowed. "No, this is an *electric* pencil sharpener. Plugs right into the wall. Nifty, right? And she's only asking a dollar. Excellent deal."

"You go through a lot of pencils, do you?"

"I do, as a matter of fact! With my word searches."

"You do word searches?"

"You don't know everything there is to know about me, Calvin."

"I guess not," Calvin said and took a sip of his coffee. Then he promptly yanked the cup away from his lip as if it had bitten him. "Ow!" he exclaimed. "Why do they have to make this so dang hot?"

As he was sticking his tongue out and fanning it with one hand, a silver F150 pulled up beside them.

"This must be her," Gertrude said, and got out of the car. "Hi," she said to the woman in the Ford. "I'm Hazel. Are you Penny?"

"I am," she said, and handed the pencil sharpener out through the window.

"Do you know Samantha Cooper?" Gertrude asked.

Penny's face scrunched up. "Don't think so," she said, still holding the pencil sharpener outstretched.

Gertrude leaned toward her, trying to see if she was lying.

"What?" Penny asked.

Gertrude pulled Samantha's photo out of her pocket. "Do you recognize this woman?"

Penny leaned away from Gertrude. "What's this about?"

"How about Martha Giles? Do you know her?"

"No. Wait. Actually, yeah. I think I've bought a few things from her before. Why?"

"Have you ever kidnapped anyone?" Gertrude asked.

"Excuse me?"

Calvin, now standing behind Gertrude, cleared his throat. Gertrude jumped. She hadn't heard him get out of the car. "Um, Hazel, why don't you give this young lady her dollar, and let her get on her way?"

Gertrude looked over her shoulder at him. "I'm just asking a few questions."

"I know." He gave her a stern look she found most annoying.

"Fine," she said, and handed the dollar through the window. Then she started to get back into Calvin's car.

"Don't you want this?" Penny asked, still holding the pencil sharpener.

"Yes, of course. I'll take that," Calvin said. "You have a nice day." Then Calvin and his new pencil sharpener got back into his car. Penny pulled away so fast, her tires squealed. "Well that was probably the most uncomfortable dollar she's ever earned," Calvin said, turning sideways to place the pencil sharpener in the backseat.

"You wanna tell me what *that* was all about?" Gertrude asked. She was so livid, her hands were shaking.

"Gertrude, you can't talk to people like that!"

"I was just asking if she was the kidnapper!"

"And what did you expect her to say, 'Why yes, as a matter of fact, I *am* the kidnapper. Now would you please be so kind as to put the handcuffs on me? But first, here's your pencil sharpener.'"

"No. *Obviously*. If she was the kidnapper, I would have expected her to lie. And then I would've known she was lying. And I would have told Hale she was the bad guy."

"OK, fine. I was just trying to help. Next time, we'll do it your way. But just so you know, you're making a fool of yourself."

"Fine," Gertrude said.

"Fine," Calvin agreed.

"I didn't even get to ask about Patsy," Gertrude muttered.

They sat there silently for a long minute. Gertrude started feeling guilty about being cross with Calvin. She kind of needed him. She didn't think Norman would sit next to the McDonald's dumpster with her. "Want to go get some milkshakes? My treat."

"Your treat?" Calvin asked, incredulous.

"Well, yes. I have a coupon."

"Then why didn't you use it on the biscuit and coffee I bought you?"

"It's not a biscuit-and-coffee coupon. It's a *milkshake* coupon. Buy one get one free."

"Do we have time before our next meet?"

"Oh yeah, plenty of time."

"Fine then," Calvin gave in. "A milkshake would be delightful."

Gertrude made no move to get out of the car.

"Well? Do I have to go in and get it?"

"No, but can you take me through the drive through?"

"Gertrude, the door is twenty feet away!"

"I know, but my back is sore. And how am I supposed to lug two milkshakes with my walker? Come on. Be a sport."

Calvin made no move to start the car.

"Pretty please with pickles on top?"

Calvin chuckled wearily. "Fine." He backed out of their spot and then rolled the car around the restaurant to get into the drive-through lane. Then he groaned. "I should've just walked in. Now we're going to miss our meet because we're stuck in line."

"Oh, stop it. We have plenty of time. Besides, there are two lanes. See?"

"That's just an illusion," Calvin said. "It doesn't make things any faster. It just makes you *think* you're moving faster."

Several minutes later, they pulled up to the squawk box. Gertrude leaned over across

Calvin's lap to stick her face out the window. He pressed himself back against the seat.

"Welcome to McDonald's! Would you like to try our new sweet potato fries?" the box said.

"No!" Gertrude hollered at the box, well beyond annoyed. "We want two small milkshakes! I have a coupon! It says B-O-G-O." She spelled it out as if she were in a spelling bee with judges who were hard of hearing.

"OK, what flavors would you like?" the box asked with an admirable lack of emotion.

Gertrude looked at Calvin, whose face was only inches from her own. "What kind do you want?" she whispered.

"Vanilla," he whispered back. "And can you get off me?"

"I'll have one vanilla shake," she hollered out the window.

"OK, and what flavor would you like for the second shake?" the box said.

Gertrude stayed where she was, not saying a word.

"Gertrude," Calvin prodded.

"What?" Gertrude asked.

"What kind do you want? We're holding up the line."

"I'm trying to decide!" she whispered to Calvin. Then she hollered at the box, "I can't decide. Can you just mix all three flavors together into one shake?"

"Yes, ma'am," the voice in the box said, as if he got this request all the time. "Please pull ahead to the first window."

Gertrude fell back into her own seat, and Calvin let out a big puff of air. He put the car in drive and rolled to the first window.

"I really wish they wouldn't call me ma'am," Gertrude said.

When they finally got back to their spot by the dumpster, Jen and her snow globe were waiting in a blue Oldsmobile.

"Aw, shucks. We're late," Gertrude said.

"I told you so."

"That'll be enough out of you," Gertrude said. "Here, hold my shake."

"There's a cup holder right there," Calvin said.

"Oh. Fancy!" Gertrude slid the shake into the slot. Then she climbed out of the car.

"Are you Hazel?" Jen was an attractive older woman whose voice was soft and grandmotherly.

"I sure am!"

"Here you go, then." Jen handed Gertrude the snow globe.

"Thanks," Gertrude said, and handed Jen the money. She was wondering if she was too tired to get through her questions when Jen broke the silence.

"Thanks for taking that off my hands. Ever since I read *Under the Dome*, my snow globes have made me nervous."

"Snow *globes*?" Gertrude repeated. "As in you have a collection?"

"Well, not anymore. That's my last one. Took a while to sell that one, on account of the giraffe's head being broken off."

Gertrude squinted into the snow globe. Sure enough, the giraffe was headless. She hadn't noticed that in the photograph online. *How does a head get chopped off* inside *a snow globe? Isn't that the safest place for a head to be?* Gertrude realized she was staring into the snow globe as if it were a crystal ball. She looked up at Jen. "Why is there a giraffe in the snow globe?"

Jen laughed. "I got it at the Boston Zoo."

"Ah, I see. So, do you know Samantha Cooper?"

"Nope, can't say as I do. Why, she a snow globe collector too?"

"Ah, no, not that I know of. How about Martha Giles?"

Jen frowned. "No. But I'm not very good with names." She shifted in her seat.

Gertrude sensed she was losing her. She pushed the next question out quickly. "Did you ever deal with anyone named Patsy Pelotte?"

A look of recognition flashed across Jen's face. "Not positive, but I did chat with someone named Patsy about the snow globes a few times. We could never coordinate a meet, though. She was always wanting to meet in weird areas after dark. Sorry, I'm just too nervous for that."

"Not nervous, just wise. You're a smart woman, Jen."

Jen smiled.

"Well, it might not be anything, but I think this Patsy lady is a bad apple, and I'm trying to track her down. Can I give you my business card, in case you think of anything else about her?"

Jen didn't look excited, but she took the outstretched card. She looked down at it, and then looked up at Gertrude. "I thought your name was Hazel?"

8

"What's next?" Calvin asked. "I'm tired already. Feels like I took a sedative. Must have been the milkshake."

"Dolly at Pine Grove Park."

Calvin looked at her. "Seriously? That's clear across town."

Gertrude shrugged. "That's where she wanted to meet. Actually, she wanted to meet there tonight, but I said we had to do it today. So apparently, she's running there on her lunch break."

Calvin grimaced. "I hate that place. Where all the druggies hang out. What does she drive?"

"I don't think there are very many druggies in Mattawooptock, and I don't know what she's driving."

Calvin looked at her again, one eyebrow raised.

"She said she didn't know what she would be driving, because she would have to borrow a vehicle from someone."

"So how are we supposed to find her?"

"She said she'd be down by the river."

"Perfect. So when she murders us, she can just throw us right in." Calvin rubbed his stomach. "You got any antacids?"

"Yessirree, hang on!" She flipped over onto her stomach so she could reach into her walker pouch in the back. Calvin leaned toward the window to distance himself from her rear.

She flopped back down into the seat and handed him a half-consumed roll of antacids. He took them tentatively. The wrapper was so worn, the brand name wasn't even visible.

"How long have these been banging around in your bag?"

"Not too long, I suppose."

"How do I even know they're antacids?"

Gertrude glared at him. "You asked me for antacids. I gave you antacids. I'm telling you they're antacids. You don't have to eat them."

"And I won't." Calvin dropped the small, well-traveled package into a cupholder.

A few minutes later, Calvin pulled the Cadillac into Pine Grove Park.

"That way," Gertrude said, pointing.

"Yes, Gertrude. I know where the river is."

"There," Gertrude said. "That must be her." A large white van sat alone in a small parking area near the river. Though, it wasn't *exactly* white. The bottom of the van was caked with mud and its tinted windows were covered in dust. Calvin pulled in beside it. Then he reached for the antacids.

"All right. Now, this one is chatty, so let me do my thing please. I'm going to get her talking."

"She was chatty online?"

"Oh Mylanta, you should've seen it! When we were setting up the meet, she wanted to play twenty questions. Thinks she's my new best friend or something."

Gertrude climbed out of the Cadillac as Dolly slid out of the van. She made Dolly wait while she wrestled her walker out of the backseat. She probably wouldn't need the walker, but her money (and her pepper spray) were in the pouch.

She unfolded her walker, leaned on it, and gave Dolly the biggest smile she could muster, but Dolly wasn't even looking at her. She was looking at Calvin, who was still sitting in the car.

"I thought you said you weren't married," Dolly said.

"Heavens, no! That's just Calvin. I'm not married. I'm Hazel," Gertrude said, and stuck her hand out.

Dolly shook it tentatively. "I see." She reached into her van and grabbed a plastic bag. "Here's your dress. Hope you like it."

"Thanks," Gertrude said, taking the dress. "Do you know Samantha Cooper?"

Dolly's upper lip twitched. "I don't think so. Why?"

Gertrude stared at her. "Just wondering. She's the one who introduced me to

VardSale, is all. And now I can't seem to get in touch with her to thank her. You know, you are an awfully skinny little thing."

"Beg your pardon?"

"Well, this dress is a size twenty, and, well, you're *not*."

"Oh, right." Dolly tittered. "Well, I buy and sell stuff. So I got this at a lawn sale, for only a quarter. Sell it to you for a dollar, and well, I've made seventy-five cents." She tittered again.

"I see how you did that math there," Gertrude said.

"OK, well, can I have that dollar?" Dolly asked.

"Sure," Gertrude said, reaching into her walker pouch. The dollar was right on top, but she pretended to dig around for it. "How about Martha Giles? Do you know her?"

Dolly's top lip twitched again. "No. Sure don't."

Gertrude stared at her closely. Something was making this woman incredibly uncomfortable.

"Patsy Pelotte?"

The color in Dolly's cheeks drained then. "You know what? I'm kind of in a hurry. Got to get back to work. Do you have that dollar?"

"Sure do." Gertrude handed it to her and smiled again. "You have a nice day now. Stay safe."

Without another word, Dolly got into her van, and drove away. Gertrude hurriedly jammed her walker into the backseat and threw herself into the front.

"Stay safe?" Calvin repeated with a chuckle.

"She's the one!" Gertrude said. "Follow her!"

Calvin sighed and made no move to follow anyone. "I heard the whole thing, Gert. She did behave a little strangely, but so did you. If she does as much business as she says she does on VardSale—"

"Calvin! Follow her!" Gertrude said, feeling frantic.

"I most certainly will not! As I was saying, if she does a lot of VardSale transactions, she might be aware there's some shady stuff going on. Maybe those women haven't responded to her messages either. Maybe she thought *you* were the bad guy."

Gertrude thought she might cry. Why had God given her such a pigheaded partner? "Calvin, puh-lease follow her! I know she's the bad guy! She was lying!"

"How do you know she was lying?"

"Start driving and I'll tell you!"

"I'll start driving, but that's just because I don't want to spend any more time in the druggie park. I'm still not following her." He put the car in drive and crawled out of the park.

Gertrude thought her head might explode. "She was lying. I just know. And did you see how unhappy she was to see you?"

"I sure did. That's the part that makes me think she's not our kidnapper. She seemed to be *afraid* of me. My guess is that most VardSalers are women, and that most of these women don't bring men along on their meets. She probably thought *I* was going to shove *her* into a trunk." After looking both ways with frustrating thoroughness, Calvin pulled out onto the main road.

The van was nowhere in sight.

Calvin continued, "Besides, did you see how petite she was? She couldn't wrestle anyone into a trunk."

"She wouldn't need to, Calvin. She has a van. Speaking of which, where in tarnation did it go?"

"But it's not her van, right? You really think she's going to kidnap people with a borrowed vehicle?"

"Tally ho!" Gertrude cried.

Calvin jumped. "What?"

"There she is! Up there! At the light!"

Calvin frowned. "OK. So there she is. So what?"

"Please, Calvin. I'm begging you. You don't have to get close to her. You don't have to speed. You don't have to catch her. Just follow her. See where she goes."

Calvin didn't respond, but he also didn't turn onto the road that led back to their trailer park. Instead, he followed the van south.

"It appears she's leaving Mattawooptock," Gertrude said.

"Well, maybe she works in Waterville."

"And she drove all the way to Pine Grove to make 75 cents? I doubt it."

"Maybe she has another sale in Waterville."

"All on a lunch break? I highly doubt it."

There was now only one vehicle between Calvin's Cadillac and Dolly's van.

"Easy does it," Gertrude said. "You don't want her to make us."

"Make us?"

"That's what Danno always says."

The van was pulling away fast.

"I didn't say slow down to a crawl," Gertrude said. "I just said don't let her see us."

"I didn't slow down at all, Gertrude. She sped up."

"Oh! Oh no! In that case, you need to speed up too!"

"Will you make up your mind?"

It was now obvious to Gertrude that Dolly was speeding. "Come on, Calvin! She's getting away!"

"I'm going 55, Gertrude! What do you want from me?"

"Don't be such an old fart! Put the hammer down!"

Calvin sped up. A little.

"Calvin!" Gertrude cried, desperate.

"Calm down, Gertrude. We're almost to Waterville now, and she'll have to slow down in town."

"No she won't!" Gertrude cried as she watched the van take a hard right onto the interstate onramp. Dolly took the corner so fast, the van appeared to tip to one side. Seconds later, Calvin took the same corner at almost the same speed.

"Eiiiii!" Gertrude cried. She was a little scared of dying. She was also having terrific fun.

Calvin straightened the car out and regained control. Dolly was just ahead. But neither Calvin nor Gertrude looked to their left before Calvin attempted to merge with traffic. And apparently there was an eighteen wheeler in the way, which promptly blew its air horn, scaring the snot out of Calvin, who yanked the car toward the shoulder. Gertrude looked to their left. The truck was so close, all she could see was the solid green side of the trailer mere inches from their car. The truck continued to blow the horn as it sped past.

Calvin took his foot off the gas and put his hand on his chest.

"Let's go!" Gertrude cried. "She's getting away!"

The Cadillac rolled to a stop. Calvin was breathing hard. "I can't, Gertrude."

"Are you having a heart attack?"

"No," Calvin said, rubbing his chest, "I'm having a Gertrude attack. Because this proves it yet again. You are going to kill me long before natural causes get me."

Gertrude leaned back in her seat. The van was already out of sight. "So we're not going after her?"

"No. We are most certainly, unequivocally, not."

"Will you at least admit now that she's suspicious?"

"Like I said, she's suspicious or we are. She might've thought she was running for her life."

"Well, she most certainly, unequivocally, wasn't."

9

When Gertrude got home, she called Hale. He wasn't available. Would she like to leave a message? "Tell him I know who the kidnapper is. Her name is Dolly Davis."

"Hold, please."

Hale picked up the phone less than a minute later.

"Screening your calls?" Gertrude asked.

"Yes. I'm a little busy here. We've got two missing women, you know. Who is Dolly Davis?"

"I found her on VardSale. *Very* shady character. Calvin insists she's innocent, but I'm telling you, she's involved somehow."

"Why does Calvin think she's innocent?"

"You'd have to ask Calvin that. I'm telling you to look into her, and I'm the gumshoe, aren't I?"

Hale snorted. "OK, I'll check her out. You got any other information on her, other than a fake-sounding name?"

Gertrude thought for a second. "She was driving a big white van that hasn't seen a carwash since the OJ trial."

Gertrude thought she heard Hale snicker. "License plate?"

"Aw, shucks, I didn't think to look at that."

"Sure, you're a gumshoe all right."

"Oh hush! It wasn't even her van. She borrowed it from a friend."

"Sure she did. Why don't you stay out of this, now, Gertrude. This is a serious case. I don't want you getting hurt."

Gertrude hung up the phone. She was furious with Hale, but she was even more furious with herself. Maybe the van wasn't borrowed. And how could she have forgotten to look at the license plate? She was suddenly exceptionally motivated to get back to work, but Calvin had said he needed a nap, and made her promise not to come back to his trailer for at least two hours. What was she going to do till then? She decided she would try to navigate VardSale on her smartphone. It would be difficult to see anything on the tiny screen, but it was better than nothing.

She sat down in her recliner and was immediately joined by a purring Hail. She scratched him beside the ear. "Who's my favorite Hail?" she cooed. "You are! Yes, you are my favorite Hail, so much nicer, so much more handsome ..."

The VardSale website finally loaded on her phone. Then a pop-up flashed, "Download the VardSale App?" *There's an app? Nifty!* She clicked download.

It took her three tries to remember her password, but soon she was logged in and scrolling. *This is great,* she thought. She decided to poke around on Dolly's profile, see if she could find anything suspicious, but she couldn't find Dolly's profile at all. *What in tarnation?* She clicked on her own messages, found Dolly's name there, and clicked on it, which led to a message: "This user account has been removed." *I knew it! She has something to hide, all right, and I made her nervous enough to delete her account. Hooray for me!*

Her first instinct was to call Hale and tell him, but then she remembered how he had implied she wasn't really a gumshoe, so she decided not to. Instead, she tried to message Dolly.

"I know who you are," she typed.

Immediately, VardSale said, "Message undeliverable. User account deleted."

Fine then. Be that way. She stared at her phone, trying to figure out what to do next. Then she remembered something Hale had said: "fake-sounding name." Patsy Pelotte was a fake name. Dolly Davis sounded like a fake name. She started to scroll through the sellers, looking for something else that sounded phony. But there were so *many* names. *This is a wild goose chase*, she thought, and then she saw it: Loretta Lenfestey. *Oh Mylanta, he was right. This looney is a country western fan.* She clicked on Loretta's profile. She only had a few items listed.

Gertrude desperately wanted to set up a meet for one of these items, but "Dolly" had already met "Hazel," so she didn't think "Loretta" would respond to "Hazel." She'd probably just delete this profile too.

Gertrude logged out and then began the process of registering for a new account. This took far longer on the small screen with her chubby fingers, and she was cursing Calvin for napping at a time like this, but finally, she had a new account. She had been tempted to name herself Tammy, after Tammy Wynette, but was afraid that might give her whole ruse away. So she went with "Jill Howe" as her new code name. A nice, normal, real-sounding name.

Then she clicked on "Set up a meet" under a decorative cutting board. One could never have too many of those. "Can we meet today?" she typed.

"Loretta" responded immediately. *Scary fast.* Gertrude hesitated to answer her. She thought it might be smarter to wait for Calvin to finish his nap, but she also knew time was of the essence. Women were in danger.

"How are you today?" Loretta asked.

Oh this is so the same wacko. "I'm great. How are you? I am very interested in your rooster cutting board. Can you meet today?"

The words "Sure can!" immediately popped up. "I see your profile says Mattawooptock. I was born and raised in Mattawooptock! How about you?"

Gertrude groaned. Enough with the twaddle. "Yes. Can we set up a meet?"

"Sure can! Do you have a big family?"

Gertrude rolled her eyes, beyond annoyed. Then she had a thought: *Two can play this game!* "I do not. Just me. Do you have a big family?"

"No. Are you married?"

"No," Gertrude typed. "Are you?"

"No, me neither. Do you have any children?"

"No." Gertrude paused, her pointer finger hovering over the small keyboard. She tried to think of some prying question to ask, something that would gain her information without making it obvious that she was trying to gain information. "How long have you been doing VardSale?" she wrote.

"Just started. Where would you like to meet?"

Hm … I might be losing her. She thought for a minute, and then typed, "Have you met any interesting people doing VardSale?"

"No. Do you want to set up a meet?"

Gertrude gave up then. She wanted to keep asking questions, but she didn't want to scare the kook off and ruin the chances of a meet. So, they ironed out the details. They would meet outside Gertrude's trailer in a half hour.

In those thirty minutes, Gertrude formed her plan. And she was certain it was a solid one. She would disguise herself, so that Patsy-Dolly-Loretta wouldn't recognize her at first. Then, when Loretta got out of the van, Gertrude would spray her with pepper spray, grab the keys out of the van's ignition, run inside, and call Hale. She would be the hero. Lives would be saved.

The first step was the disguise. She had to change her clothes. Loretta had already seen her in her current snazzy outfit. So, she put on a sleeveless pink romper, which cooled her off immensely. *I should've just worn this in the first place.* Next, she found a hat. She had many to choose from, and she went with a large straw number that would cover most of her face *and* keep the sun off her pale shoulders. Now, for glasses. She had a large collection of reading glasses, and she picked the flashiest ones—a pair of emerald cat-eyes. Then she went to the door and waited.

As she waited, a thought occurred to her. *The walker.* It might give her away. *But I need it.* But did she really? Could she make it all the way out to the driveway, pepper spray a person, grab some keys, and make it back inside without her walker? *Maybe I can. I'll have a good dose of adrenaline on my side.* She took the pepper spray out of her walker pouch and slid it into the right pocket of her romper. She put her phone in her left pocket and then took a deep breath. *No. There's no way. I have to take the walker.* But Loretta would recognize it. Loretta was no dummy, or she would've already been caught. *I can't.* She had to.

The same ominous dirty white van pulled up alongside Gertrude's trailer. *Borrowed, my butt! Hale was right!* She hated it when Hale was right. She looked down at her walker. Then she opened the door, and stepped outside without it.

She kept her head down, looking at her steps. She wobbled a little, but this was mostly because her new glasses were making her vision all wonky, and only a little because of the missing walker.

The fingers of her right hand were curled tightly around the pepper spray in her pocket. Her left hand white-knuckled the porch railing. Even without looking, she realized Loretta wasn't getting out of the van. This wasn't good. She wanted so badly to look up and make sure it was the same woman, before she blinded her, but it had to be. It was the same van.

Gertrude stepped off her bottom step and onto the spongy spring ground.

"Jill?" the woman called out hesitantly.

Gertrude tried to disguise her voice. "That's me!" she chirped. She was trying to sound harmless; instead she sounded like an old crone who had just inhaled some helium.

Then she heard the van door creak as it opened. *That's better. Come on, girl.* She saw Loretta's feet hit the ground.

Slow and steady, I'm almost there. She felt so naked without her walker, but her feet were still beneath her. She was only two feet from Loretta. *Now!* She looked up, so her aim would be true. Her right hand flew out of her romper pocket, and she aimed the poison right at Loretta's eyes.

"You!" Loretta cried.

Gertrude pressed the trigger.

And nothing happened.

She pressed the button again.

Nothing.

"You!" Loretta cried again.

"Dangonit!" Gertrude screamed. *That will teach me to buy pepper spray at a lawn sale.* She threw the small canister at Loretta's face and turned to run inside. But Loretta was already on her. Like some kind of crazy monkey, she had leapt onto Gertrude's back, and had wrapped her left arm around Gertrude's neck.

Gertrude choked at the pressure, tried to run forward, and tried to shake her off her back all at the same time. Instead, she just fell forward, the weight of Loretta driving her into the ground. Her forehead drove into the soft mud of spring, and Gertrude had a moment to silently bemoan the crushing and soiling of her straw hat brim.

"Calvin!" Gertrude tried to scream, but it came out a raspy whisper. She couldn't even breathe.

Gertrude thrashed around, trying to throw the crazy country western fan off her back. Pain shot down her left leg, which only infuriated her further. She drove her right elbow back into soft flesh, and she heard Loretta gasp in pain. She also felt Loretta's right arm leave the struggle. She wasn't sure why this was happening, but she wanted to capitalize on it. She began to flop back and forth, trying to gain some momentum so that she could eventually roll over. But the more she flopped, the tighter that left arm went around her neck.

Then she felt soft cloth being pressed over her nose and mouth. She shook her head wildly back and forth, trying to get away from it. It smelled both sweet and gross at the same time, a combination that she wouldn't have thought possible before then, and a combination she was sure couldn't be good. She opened her mouth as wide as she could and then chomped down on the cloth, trying desperately to bite the hand that held it.

Loretta didn't even flinch.

Completely out of breath, Gertrude couldn't help but inhale. She threw another right elbow, but she could tell it was too weak to do any damage. She tried to throw another, tried to kick her feet, tried to fight, but it all turned to nothing.

10

Gertrude woke up in back of the van with the worst headache of her life. It felt like someone had hit her between the eyes with an ax. She brought one hand to her head, just to make sure it was still there.

She looked around the dimly lit interior. It was still daylight, but the tinted, not to mention filthy, windows didn't allow much light into the van. The seats had been removed, and Gertrude was on the floor, which made the bumpiness of the road that much more painful. *What are we on, a skidder trail?* She sat up and looked out the windows. It did indeed appear that they were on a skidder trail. In the middle of the forest. *This van is bouncing around like a fart in a mitten.*

"Oh good, you're awake," Loretta said.

Gertrude looked up to meet her eyes in the rearview mirror. "Where are we?"

"Don't you worry, friend. The scary part is over. We are going home now."

Home? Does that mean she's going to kill me? "Are you going to kill me?"

"Kill you? Of course not! I wouldn't hurt a fly. You're my friend. I won't hurt you again. I'm sorry I hurt you at all. I wasn't planning on inviting you to come with me, at least not until I got to know you better, but then I thought maybe you knew what I was doing, and I just can't allow myself to get in trouble with the law. Not after all I've done, all I've accomplished, how far I've come."

"What you've accomplished? What have you accomplished, exactly?"

"Oh, you'll see," Loretta burbled. "You're going to love it. I promise."

She hit a giant rock with the right front tire, and Gertrude was thrown to the left wall of the van. "Ow!" she said accusingly.

"Oh, sorry, friend. I always forget that rock is there." She tittered.

Gertrude had a thought, and her hand flew to her neck, but there was nothing there. She groped around her chest, but her LifeRescue pendant was gone. Either it had fallen off in the struggle, or this madwoman had taken it. *I hate her*, Gertrude thought. *I really, really hate this lunatic.* "I'm not your friend," Gertrude snarled.

"Oh, sure you are. You just don't know it yet. You'll see. So, friend, what is your real name? I'm guessing it's not Hazel or Jill?"

"What's your name?" Gertrude asked.

"That's a fair question, I suppose. My name is Sue. Just plain old Sue. Ugliest name in the books. Not Susan, not Suzanne, just Sue. My mother was a cruel woman."

"At least you're not a boy named Sue."

Sue laughed as if that was the funniest thing she'd ever heard.

"Where are we going, Sue?"

"I told you. We are going home. And once you get settled in, if you want me to go back for a few of your cats, I would be happy to."

"How do you know I have cats?" *You'd better stay away from my cats, you wacko!*

"I saw them in your windows."

"What else did you see?"

"Nothing. Your trailer park was calm, empty, quiet. No one saw us, don't you worry."

"I was wearing a necklace. Did you take it?"

"You mean your LifeRescue button? Yes, we left that back there. Didn't want you to be tempted to press it. It probably wouldn't even work now. Not many cell phone towers up here." She giggled like a little girl.

Gertrude slumped back against the wall of the van. "How did you ever get me into this van?"

"I'm stronger than I look. Plus, there's that." Her eyes flitted to the wheelchair lift. "Now, what's your name?"

"Gertrude."

Both her hands left the wheel and came together in a delighted little double clap. "Gertrude! What a wonderful name! It suits you! Much better than Hazel or Jill."

"I am Gertrude, Gumshoe, and the cops know all about you. They know what you drive. I even gave them your license plate."

Sue tittered again. "Well, then, I guess I'd better not go back for any cats! Why don't you lie down and rest? There's not much to see around here but trees, and we've got about another hour to go."

"Another hour? Where are we going, Canada?"

Sue didn't answer. Gertrude tried to figure out what time it was. *My phone!* she remembered. She still wasn't used to having a phone with her at all times. She reached into her pocket. "Where's my phone?!"

"Oh don't worry, Gert. May I call you Gert? You won't need a phone where we're going. And like I said, no cell towers—"

"No, you may not call me Gert, and"— Gertrude was grinding her teeth so hard her jaw hurt—"where are you taking me?"

"Just be patient, Gertrude. You'll see soon enough."

"I have to pee," Gertrude lied.

Sue looked at her in the rearview. "Can you hold it?"

"Sure can't, Sue."

"All right. Let me think." She kept driving. Gertrude kept bouncing.

"There's not much to think about. Pull over so I can pee."

"I'm sorry. I just don't trust you, Gertrude. I'm hoping we can build trust over time. But right now, well, you gave me quite a fight back there. I don't want to have to go chasing you through the forest. And even more importantly, I don't want to have to shoot you."

"Shoot me? You have a gun?"

Sue looked at her in the rearview. "Of course I have a gun."

"I thought we were friends!" Gertrude began scanning the back of the van for a means of escape. She scooted toward the door.

"Don't even try it. It's locked."

Gertrude felt panic rising in her throat. *Calvin will tell Hale*, she told herself.

"Where's my phone?" she asked again.

"I told you, you won't need it where we're go—"

96

"I know. I heard you the first time. I'm asking *where* is my phone. Do you still have it?"

"Don't be silly. I don't want anyone tracking your phone to where we're going. And when we get there, you won't want that either. You're going to be so happy, Gertrude! Don't you worry."

"So, *where is the phone exactly?*"

"In the mud. Right beside that ugly hat of yours."

"That hat wasn't ugly! You're going to pay for that!"

"For the insult, or for the hat?"

"Both!"

So Hale will find the phone, and maybe it will have this lunatic's fingerprints on it. Please hurry, Hale. She couldn't believe she was betting the farm on Hale.

11

Finally, the van stopped.

"Where are we?" All Gertrude could see was woods.

"Almost home. Here, put this on." Sue handed her a pillowcase.

"Are we going to a three-legged race?"

Sue laughed. "No, silly. I want you to put it on over your head. Just for a few minutes. We need to walk now, and I don't want you knowing where the van is."

Gertrude's whole body went cold with panic. "Walk? I can't walk! I don't have my walker!"

"Your walker?" Sue frowned. "I thought that was part of your first disguise. You didn't have it when you came out of the trailer."

"That's 'cause I only had to take ten steps! I can't hike through the woods! I'm disabled!"

"I'll help you," she said. "Put the pillowcase on." Sue turned around in her seat, and Gertrude saw the revolver in her lap.

Reluctantly, Gertrude took the pillowcase from her hands. She didn't want to put it on, but she also wanted to get out of the van. Her back was killing her, and now she really did have to pee. She slid the pillowcase over her head. It smelled like lavender.

"There. Now you happy?" Gertrude snarled.

Sue didn't answer her. Gertrude heard her get out of the van, and then a few seconds later, she heard the back door open. The van filled with light. *Aha! I can see light through this thing! Bet you didn't know that!*

"OK, easy does it now, I don't want you to hurt yourself. Just ease on out of the van. I've got you."

Gertrude scooted her butt toward the door, and then she felt a hand on her arm. "You don't have to squeeze so tight," she hissed.

"Just trying to help," Sue said in a voice so light she might have been planning a tea party for fairies.

Gertrude's feet hit the ground, and her legs filled with tingling. She realized her knees were knocking and willed them to stop. *I sure do wish I had more faith in Hale.* Her first step left her unscathed, but on her second, her toe caught on something hard and she tumbled forward.

Sue caught her. "There, there, easy does it."

"How am I supposed to walk if I can't see my feet?"

"You'll be all right. Pick your feet up when you walk. Just go slow. I've got you. I'm not going to let you run into a tree."

"Oh no, but you'll shoot me?"

"I don't want to shoot you, Gertrude. I want us to be friends. Now walk."

Gertrude picked her right leg up as high as it would go and then put it down three inches in front of her.

"No need to be sarcastic," Sue said.

"How can I be sarcastic with my legs?"

"Body language can be sarcastic. Now walk."

Gertrude had no idea what Sue was talking about, but then she reasoned, crazy people don't always make sense. Gertrude could see that most of the light was coming from her right. Since it must be closing in on sunset, she figured they were walking south, and she began counting her steps.

12

"We're here!" Sue sang. "You can take your hood off."

Gertrude did, and then squinted as her eyes adjusted. She smoothed out her hair and surveyed her surroundings. They were standing in a small clearing in the woods, in the middle of which stood a small cabin. Behind the cabin was a small pond. *Good. Maybe I'll get to drown her.*

Gertrude looked at Sue, who was standing uncomfortably close to her. Gertrude thought about punching her in the nose, but Sue was still holding the gun, and Gertrude already knew she was a scrappy little thing.

"Go ahead in," Sue said, nodding toward the door. "Let's meet the others."

Gertrude took a deep breath and then, holding the rickety railing at her side, climbed the few steps to the front door. She had never needed her walker so badly in her whole life.

She opened the heavy wooden door and stepped inside to find a whole host of women staring at her. It seemed there were more women in the cabin than there actually were, because the cabin was so small.

"Everyone, this is Gertrude, our new friend!"

Directly in front of Gertrude was a small, round wooden table. Around the table sat three women playing cards. The youngest of the three was exceptionally attractive, and Gertrude recognized her immediately. "Samantha?"

Samantha looked shocked, and slowly nodded.

"It's going to be all right, Samantha. Andy and the cops are looking for—"

Sue pointed the gun at Gertrude's head. "We don't talk about our former lives here. We only live in the present here. The happy, peaceful present, where we all live together, in harmony. Isn't that right, friends?"

The women nodded.

"Now, it seems you know Samantha. This wonderful woman to her left is May. And to the right of Samantha is Doris. Say hi, ladies."

"Hi," May and Doris said.

"And on the couch is Barbara, Martha, and Deborah." The couch was pushed against the far wall, which wasn't very far away at all. Each of the women held a paperback. Each meekly said hello.

Beside the couch was a doorway to a screened-in porch. Two women were standing in that doorway, looking at Gertrude. "That's Agnes and Betsy over there," Sue said pointing. "Betsy is my besty!" she quipped and then laughed maniacally.

Another woman was lying on a cot that stood against the wall to Gertrude's left.

"And that is Ruth!" Sue said, pointing at Ruth.

"Hi, everybody," Gertrude said tentatively. "Uh, why are you all just sitting—"

Samantha caught Gertrude's eye and slowly shook her head. Gertrude closed her mouth.

"They're just relaxing," Sue said. "Go ahead! Join them."

"You want me to ..." Gertrude looked around as her brain tried to make sense of what it was seeing. "... relax? So ... you took all these women? And everybody's still ... alive?"

Sue cackled crazily. "Of *course* they're all alive! They're my friends! I don't kill my friends! Now, make yourself comfortable. I'll go get you a cot and some blankets." Sue disappeared into a room to their left.

"Actually, I'd really like to use the bathroom," Gertrude called after her.

"Go ahead, Gertrude!" Sue called back. "Make yourself at home!"

The bathroom wasn't big enough to turn around in. The only window was the size of a bread box. There would be no squeezing through that exit.

When Gertrude rejoined them in the main room, the women seemed to have already forgotten about her. No one watched her as she hobbled toward the table. Doris had vacated the seat beside Samantha, and Gertrude collapsed into it. "Come on," she whispered. "Let's make a break for it."

"Now?" Samantha whispered.

"Yes, now. She's not looking."

"Look, I realize you just got here, but that is a *dumb* idea. She would chase us, she knows the area, I don't, I'm assuming you don't, and she has a gun. Besides, I'm not leaving them with her."

"We could send help."

"You're not listening. I'm not leaving them alone with a crazy lady with a gun."

Gertrude sighed and looked around. "What's in there?" Gertrude whispered, nodding toward the room Sue had disappeared into.

"Sue's bedroom."

Gertrude studied the opposite side of the cabin. "You are considerably younger than most of the women here, Samantha. Any idea why that is?"

Samantha rubbed her chest, as if she was suffering from a particularly nasty case of heartburn. "She said that she didn't plan on taking me, but then I was so 'nice and friendly' that she couldn't resist. That will teach me to be friendly."

Gertrude smirked. "So she just brings women here, and then what? We just hang out being her *friends*?" Gertrude had a sudden horrifying thought. "Samantha, did all these women come from *VardSale*?"

"That's right," Sue said from behind her.

"Jumping hot beans!" Gertrude said. "You are a sneaky one, aren't you, Sue?"

"VardSale is the perfect place to meet people. You get to feel them out first, see if they are someone you want to spend time with. But I think I'm done collecting friends for now. It seems you've attracted the attention of law enforcement, so we're just going to stay put for a while. Aren't we, ladies? Your cot is right over there," Sue said, pointing, "and I have more blankets if you need them, but it's been warm, so one should be enough for now. When you want to lie down, set your cot up where you like, but when you get up, please fold up your cot. We are limited on space around here! And you've found the bathroom, so that's good. We ask you to limit your showers to two minutes. Our hot water tank is a teeny little thing, isn't it, ladies?" She cackled again. "We've got a garden out back, so there'll be plenty of food, but if you need anything else, just let me know. I make a supply run every once in a while."

"A supply run to where?" Gertrude asked.

"The nearest town."

"Which is where?"

Sue smiled and patted Gertrude on the shoulder. "Don't you worry about that, dear. You just relax."

"Are we allowed to go outside?"

"Of course! It's beautiful out there! You can kayak on the pond, or go for a walk. Soon the water will be warm enough for swimming, and then maybe we won't need to take so many showers!" The crazy laugh again. That noise was really starting to grate on Gertrude's nerves.

"What do you say, Samantha? Want to show me around?" Gertrude asked, trying to sound peppy. "Outside?" she added for clarification.

Samantha looked at Sue as if for permission.

"Go ahead, dear. Just be back in time for supper. Now,"—she turned toward the rest of the women and clapped her hands twice rapidly—"whose turn is it to cook, anyway?"

13

There was a picnic table near the shore. Gertrude sat at it, grimacing.

"You OK?" Samantha asked.

"No. I'm not. I think my back is broken, and I'm not used to walking without my walker. I'm exhausted. And I really miss my cats." *She didn't want to admit it, but she missed Calvin too.* She slid the photo she had snagged from Samantha's bedroom mirror across the table.

Samantha peeked at it, her eyes filling with tears, and then she slid it into her pocket. "Thanks," she mumbled.

"We need to figure out a way to get out of here."

Samantha groaned. "You think we haven't thought of that? There's no way to get away, there's nowhere to go!" Samantha spread her arms. "I mean, where are we? You want me to lead a bunch of old ladies into the forest? I don't even know what state we're in! We could be in Canada for all I know!"

Gertrude thought for a minute. Then she looked at Samantha. "You're a hiker, right? So you're pretty good at finding your way around in the woods."

Samantha sighed and sat down across from Gertrude. She looked out at the water. "I'm a hiker, yes, but I hike on *trails*. I don't just go out into the tickletuppy and follow the moss and stars."

"Might be better than staying here," Gertrude muttered.

"Oh yeah? You talk tough, but what are you going to say when the sun goes down and we're out there"—she looked toward the forest—"with no bed, no food, no light?"

"She doesn't have flashlights?"

"Nope. I've looked. So ..." She looked down at her hands. "Andy? Is he OK?"

"Yes. He's worried sick. He hired me to help find you."

"He hired you?!" Samantha looked appalled. "No offense," she added hastily.

"Plenty taken. But don't get too discouraged. He called the cops too. It just took a while for them to listen to him, but they did, finally. They're looking for you. But let's take notice that it was *me*, despite your lack of confidence, who actually found you."

"Yeah, you found me all right. Now what?"

Wowsa. Super grateful. "Now we escape."

"There is no escape! There is only wait-to-be-rescued. These women are old. You're not exactly young yourself! How old *are* you, anyway?"

Gertrude ignored the question. "So you go. I'll protect them while you're gone. Then you send help."

Samantha snorted. "Yeah, you'll protect them. How do you plan to do that, without a weapon?"

"Fine. Then I'll go. You stay here and protect them."

Samantha gave her a deadly glare. "Don't you dare. Don't you dare put all of these women in danger just because you're nuts."

"Fine then. It's settled. We have to go together. All of us."

"Right. Which is impossible."

"Has anyone tried to steal the van?"

"Not that I know of, but if any of us so much as heads in that direction, she gets suspicious and follows us. Also, the van key is always in her pocket. And before you ask, she sleeps with the door locked."

"So we go outside and come into the bedroom through a window."

"Locked."

"So we break the window."

"Gun."

Gertrude paused.

"Look, I don't mean to be disrespectful, but I've been here for two days, and I'm no dummy. There *is* no way out of here. If there was, I would have thought of it."

"But Samantha, it's *ten against one*. We can do this. I'm telling you. We just need to work together."

They sat there quietly for several minutes, each lost in thought, staring out at the pond.

"You said the cops know about us, right? So aren't they coming?"

Gertrude was torn. She wanted to encourage Samantha and tell her help was on the way, but she also wanted Samantha to help her escape. She didn't want to wait around for Hale to figure things out. "Well, yes, they know. But they only know that two women are missing. And they have no idea where we are. Or who Sue is. Yes, they will probably figure it out eventually, but I don't want to stay here till winter." Gertrude paused, suddenly afflicted by a horrible thought. "What *is* her plan for winter? What is she going to do with all her 'friends' when her skidder trail fills with snow? When her water and her precious garden freezes?"

"We've discussed that too. And we don't know what she's planning. Maybe she'll let us go. Maybe she'll do something else." Samantha looked at her somberly.

"What about poison?" Gertrude whispered.

"For her or for us?"

"That's not funny. For her, of course."

"We don't have anything poisonous."

"There's got to be something poisonous out there," Gertrude said, nodding to the forest. "Mushrooms or berries?"

"Do *you* know which mushrooms and berries are poisonous?"

"Course not."

"Well, then, you'd better keep thinking."

Gertrude thought. But not for long. "We're just going to have to jump her."

"Jump her?" Samantha sounded skeptical.

"Yep. First, we let others in on the plan, all sneaky like. Then, I'll try to get behind her. You just keep your eyes on me. When I give you the signal, I'll grab her gun arm, and you punch her in the face as hard as you can."

Samantha laughed. "I don't know how to punch someone!"

"Don't you watch television? You just swing your fist through the air, while keeping your eye on the prize."

"Oh yeah? You punched a lot of people in the face?"

"As a matter of fact, yes. I punched a stripper serial killer in the face while recording her confession for the police!"

"Seriously?"

"Seriously."

"Wouldn't I have heard about a stripper serial killer in the news?"

"All right, maybe she wasn't *exactly* a serial killer. Yet. She only killed one person, but still, I'm the one who caught her. That part's as true as sunshine."

"OK," Samantha said, leaning toward her. "This is seriously a crazy idea, but I'm going crazy being here, so why not? And I know that some of these women need to see a doctor. But I think you should be the one to do the punching, since you have so much experience. And I think we should wait till morning. Sue is always a bit groggy before her coffee. I'll tell everyone tonight. Then, in the morning, first thing, as soon as she steps out of the bedroom, I'll grab her right arm, her *gun* arm, and you punch her in the face. And I'll ask all the other ladies to jump on her then too. Man, I wish we had some rope."

Gertrude burst into laughter.

"What?" Samantha asked.

"You just look so excited! This is going to be great fun!"

"Yeah. It just might be," Samantha said thoughtfully.

"Vines," Gertrude said.

"Vines?"

"Yes. Right now. You go in and distract her, and I'll go get some vines out of the woods. We'll use those to tie her up."

Samantha's eyes grew wide. "That's a great idea!"

"I know. All my ideas are great. Now go."

Samantha climbed the short slope to the cabin and disappeared inside. Gertrude took a deep breath and then stood up on shaky legs and slowly made her way to the woods.

Finding some vines was the easy part. Getting them out of the ground was not. Gertrude squatted, lost her balance, and promptly landed on her fanny, which turned out to be a fabulous turn of events. She was really quite comfortable in that position, but then she saw a spider a few inches away and decided she wouldn't stay long. She pulled on a long horizontal stem that she assumed was part of a vine, and it came up easily, but it just kept coming up. She got her feet back under her and followed the vine, hand over hand, still pulling it out of the ground, until she had about eight feet. Then she stood up straight and gave the vine a firm yank, hoping that would break it, but all this did was hurt her hands. She twisted the vine around her hand and pulled even harder. "Ow!" she cried. She stepped on the vine with her foot and then yanked with both hands, but the dang thing wouldn't break. She stooped a little and began to gnaw through it with her teeth. It tasted like the white stuff inside a grapefruit. She gagged, and then kept chewing.

Finally, she had a vine. She coiled it up and then shoved it down the front of her romper, tucking most of it into the waistband of her undies. Then she went to work on vine number two, praying those vines weren't poisonous. She didn't want to die with plants down her pants. That would be embarrassing.

When Sue called her from the house, she was gnawing through vine number three. She hurriedly stowed this one with the others and then made her way out of the woods, steadying herself on trees as she went.

When she stepped into the clearing, Sue was staring at her from the back steps. "Everything all right?" Sue called out.

"Right as rain!" Gertrude called back. "I was just exploring."

Sue stood there silently until Gertrude finally made her way to the back door. Then Sue put a hand on Gertrude's arm. "It's all right, Gertrude. Most of the ladies go through this when they first arrive, looking for a way to get away. But there really isn't anywhere to go, Gertrude. And I think you'll find that this place will grow on you. Soon, you won't even want to leave!"

Gertrude summoned up her best poppycock smile. Then she patted Sue's hand. "You're right, Sue. I think it already is growing on me. It's so beautiful. So peaceful. Why don't you call me Gert."

Sue's face spread into a giant smile, and she flung her arms around Gertrude, one hand still holding the revolver. Gertrude wasn't expecting this, and she grabbed the doorframe to steady herself.

"There, there," Gertrude said, patting the lunatic on the back.

14

When Gertrude reentered the cabin, everyone turned to stare at her. But the stares were different this time. They all knew. They all knew the plan. Samantha had already spread the word. *Good girl, Samantha. Andy was right about you.* Gertrude gave them a small smile and then said, "What smells so yummy?"

Martha had made stir fry for supper, and it did smell delicious. Gertrude realized she was famished. She'd been so busy, she'd plumb forgotten all about food.

Gertrude gobbled up her share and then wished for more, but alas, none was forthcoming. She vowed to eat till she was full as a tick the next night, when she was safe at home with her cats.

She jumped. *I can't believe my cats will be home alone all night*. She hadn't spent an entire night away from them since they had moved into that trailer. She hoped they wouldn't worry. Then she remembered they were cats, and that they would be fine. She was the one who wasn't fine.

After the plates were cleared and the dishes done, Sue clapped her hands twice and said, "Who's up for a game of Monopoly?" A few women dutifully made their way to the table.

Gertrude went to the small bookshelf, grabbed a random paperback, and then went to sit next to Samantha. "We good?" she muttered as she opened the book.

"Mm-hmm," Samantha murmured. "But your book is upside down."

Gertrude looked. Indeed it was. She flipped it over and pretended to read.

The women were still deep in the throes of real estate war when Gertrude stretched out on her cot. *I'll never be able to fall asleep*, she thought, *I'll just rest my eyes for a bit*. And then Gertrude promptly zonked out.

The next thing she knew, someone was placing a hand over her mouth. She awoke with a start and tried to swat away the hand, but then she saw Samantha's gentle face hovering over hers, the pointer finger of her free hand in front of her lips. Gertrude nodded, understanding, and Samantha slowly withdrew her hand from Gertrude's mouth.

Gertrude squinted to look around the dark room. Almost everyone else was awake, though it was still dark out.

"What time is it?" Gertrude whispered.

Samantha's finger flew back into the "sh" position, and then she whispered, "It's time." She got up to wake up the few women who were still sleeping. She woke each of them in the same eerie manner, and one by one, the women sat up.

Gertrude felt them staring at her and was suddenly resentful that they all seemed to be counting on her. *I didn't ask for this*, she thought, but then realized that yes, she had. This is exactly what she had asked for. She decided she was retiring from the gumshoe business. There was just too much pressure.

The last woman woken, Samantha tiptoed to her spot beside Sue's door. Everyone else lay back down, but their eyes were wide open, and Gertrude could tell, even in the dim light, that their bodies were rigid with readiness.

Gertrude got up and stood on the other side of the door. Then she thought better of it. This wasn't a very good angle from which to throw a punch. She decided to instead squat behind the table. Then she could come at Sue straight on, like a giant bowling ball.

The minutes seemed to stretch, and the sun came up, slowly filling the cabin with light. Gertrude's left leg fell asleep, and she shifted her weight. Yep, definitely retiring. She realized she was holding her breath and tried to take slow, even breaths. She wished she had a cat to pet.

Finally, Gertrude heard rustling inside Sue's room, and she saw Samantha stand up straighter. Gertrude got ready to pounce. And then they waited. And they waited. And the door didn't open. Gertrude didn't dare relax, though, and it was a good thing, because when the door opened, it flew open.

Sue stepped out boldly and began to say, "Good morning!" but Samantha cut her sunrise greeting short by grabbing her right arm and twisting it hard behind Sue's back.

"Ow!" Sue cried, sounding more offended than injured.

Gertrude leapt out from behind the table and ran at Sue, full steam ahead. Sue saw her coming and her eyes just had time to go wide before Gertrude's chubby little fist slammed into the side of Sue's jaw, and her eyes shut. She whimpered, and started to fall to her right. Samantha helped her get the rest of the way to the floor. Then women from all over the room descended on her, pinning her to the rough wooden boards beneath her.

"Grab the gun!" Samantha cried. It had fallen out of Sue's pocket, but Sue didn't even seem to be aware of that fact. She just lay there sobbing. Gertrude grabbed the gun and pointed it at her. She felt herself smile. *This is kind of fun.* Her back hurt, her fist hurt, her knees hurt from squatting behind the table, but she was actually having fun. She was so *not* retiring. Holding the gun steady, Gertrude reached into her romper and withdrew the vines. She threw them into the fray. "Hogtie her, girls!"

It took the women several minutes to untangle the vines, and when they did, they didn't hogtie anything. Martha daintily tied Sue's hands, while Agnes politely tied her feet. But it didn't matter. Sue was not trying to get away. The only movement coming from her body were the tears sliding out of her eyes and down her cheeks.

"Is she all right?" Betsy the besty asked.

"She's fine," Samantha said.

"Shouldn't we let her go to the bathroom?" May asked.

"Seriously?" Samantha said.

May looked down at Sue, crumpled on the floor. "Well, she just woke up, and we're going to leave her here, right? All tied up? Shouldn't we at least let her use the bathroom first?"

They all stood there silently, looking down at their captor, appearing to think over May's suggestion.

"She *kidnapped* us," Samantha reminded them.

"I'll do it," Dorothy said. "I used to be a nurse. I'll take her." Then she looked at Samantha. "Can you help her up?"

Samantha rolled her eyes, but she helped Sue up and to the bathroom. Sue and Dorothy wouldn't both fit into the small room, so they left the door open. All the women turned around, so as to give them some privacy.

They heard a flush, and then Sue said, "Thank you, dear friends."

What an absolute fruitcake, Gertrude thought.

Samantha helped her sit back down, her back against the wall.

"Samantha, do we have the van key?" Gertrude asked, eager to get this show on the road.

Samantha's brow furrowed. She reached into Sue's pocket and then her face relaxed with relief. She tossed a set of keys to Gertrude.

Gertrude tried to catch them, but they bounced off her ample chest and landed on the floor.

"Good stop," Samantha said.

"That'll be enough out of you, wise guy." Gertrude grunted as she bent over to retrieve the keys. "Is she tied up tight?"

Samantha gave the vines a good tug. "Seems to be."

"Let's go then." Gertrude opened the front door of the cabin and started shooing women outside. "We'll send you help, Sue," Gertrude added, and then stepped outside, pulling the door shut behind her.

The women were standing clustered in the clearing, looking up at Samantha and Gertrude.

"Let's go," Gertrude said.

"We don't know which way to go," Dorothy said.

"We go north," Gertrude said. "Just keep the sun to your right."

"We can't see the sun," Dorothy said.

Oh Mylanta, Gertrude thought in exasperation. "It's right there," she said, pointing to the brightest area of the dawn sky.

They started walking. Gertrude turned around to look back every few steps, but there was no one behind them.

"How far is it?" Samantha asked.

"Sh, I'm counting." They walked in silence for several minutes, Gertrude once again longing for her walker, and then she abruptly stopped.

"What is it?" Samantha stopped too.

"That's it. We should be here." Gertrude looked around. "That was 543 steps."

"OK, well then, we're close. Ladies,"— Samantha turned her attention to the rest of the women—"we are close. Fan out a little and look for the van, but don't lose sight of one another in the process." She looked at Gertrude. "It's OK, Gertrude. You did it. You got us out. We're almost home free."

The women spread out to look. Gertrude sat on a log and kept watch against spiders.

In just a few minutes, a woman called out, "I found the road!"

The rest of the women hurried to the sound of her voice, and sure enough, there was the road.

"Which way?" Deborah asked, panting.

"That way." Gertrude pointed.

"Isn't that back toward the cabin, though?" Deborah asked, her voice sounding tired and scared.

"Yes, but it's also toward the van. You can walk the other way, if you want," Gertrude said. "We'll pick you up when we go by."

"Can we just wait here?" Deborah asked. "We're not all young pups like you."

Gertrude smiled. "Of course. You girls take a break. We'll go fetch the van."

Gertrude and Samantha headed up the road. "You know," Samantha muttered, "you can stay here too. I know you miss your walker. I can go get the van."

"No way, José. Deborah just called me young."

Samantha laughed.

"You have a pretty laugh, Samantha."

"Thank you, Gertrude."

They rounded a corner, and there it sat.

"Tally ho!" Gertrude cried.

Samantha groaned. "I hate that thing."

"Me too," Gertrude said, and handed her the keys.

Samantha took them. "You don't want to drive?"

Gertrude put her hands on her hips. "Not that it matters on this road, but I don't exactly have a driver's license."

Samantha frowned. "What kind of a private investigator doesn't have a driver's license?"

15

It wasn't easy loading those tired, sore, scared women into the back of a seatless van. One by one, Samantha and Gertrude helped them up and in. Most of them were able to sit on the floor. Ruth said it hurt to sit, so she lay down, resting her head on Martha's lap.

Gertrude and Samantha climbed into the front, and Samantha put the keys in the ignition. She turned the key. The van started. Samantha let out a big puff of air.

"Were you not expecting it to start?"

Samantha shook her head and put the van in reverse. "I had my doubts. So far this whole escape has seemed a little too good to be true." The van was pointed in the wrong direction, so Samantha had to do some creative maneuvering to get it turned around in the narrow road, which was really more of a path. Finally, the van was pointed south.

"And we're off like a terd of hurdles," Gertrude said triumphantly.

"What?" Samantha asked.

"I said, we're off like a herd of turtles. It's an expression."

"Except that's not what you said."

Gertrude gave her a dirty look. "You're not making any sense, Samantha. But it's all right. I know you've been through a lot. You're not used to the crime-fighting life like I am."

Samantha drove over the muddy, bumpy one-lane road for over an hour before she reached an intersection. The van rolled to a stop. She groaned and put her head on the steering wheel. "Now what," she muttered.

Gertrude looked around. "Straight ahead looks like it gets traveled more often. Let's try that one."

Samantha looked up. "What if it doesn't go anywhere?"

"We're traveling south, Samantha. We'll get somewhere eventually."

Samantha pushed on the gas pedal. "What the heck. Maybe we'll get to Mexico. I could use a Corona."

They drove for another hour, and finally reached an intersection with an actual road. It was still gravel, but it looked maintained. "Which way, now?"

Gertrude pointed to the right. "South."

Samantha turned right.

"How's the gas gauge?" Gertrude asked.

"An eighth of a tank."

"It'll be all right. We're on a real road now. Someone will find us eventually."

Now that they were on a smooth road, Gertrude had trouble keeping her eyes open. She started to nod off and then felt guilty, as she was all comfy up front, while the other women were crammed in the back. She forced herself to open her eyes. And that's when she saw it. "Look!" she cried, pointing.

Samantha gasped. "What is that?"

"It's a building!"

"Well, I can see that, but what kind of a building?"

"It looks like a house."

"But who has a house way out here? What if it's a relative of Sue's?"

"First of all, that's not funny. Second, I've still got the gun. You just go knock on the door. I'll cover you."

"OK." She pulled the big clunker into the short driveway, and climbed out of the van. The women in the back all pressed against the windows to watch.

Samantha didn't even get to knock. A man met her on the porch. Gertrude leaned out her window to try to hear what they were saying, but she couldn't hear a word. Still, the man looked friendly enough, and Samantha's posture seemed to be relaxing. Soon, she was headed back toward the van, smiling.

"He says he'll call the police, but it will take them a while to get here, so we can go inside if we want. He says he's got more guns than God, and he'll let us use them if she comes after us."

"Really? He's going to arm the Red Hats Society?"

Samantha blinked in confusion.

"Never mind. Did he say where we are?"

"Yep. He said we're in 5R11. Not even a real town."

"Does he live here?"

"Says it's his vacation home."

"Hm. Well, that's suspicious." Gertrude looked over her shoulder at all the nervous faces. "You girls want to get out of the van?"

Samantha opened the back door, and the women slowly tumbled out. Samantha had to help most of them, but getting them out was far easier than getting them in had been. There was a lot of stretching and a little crying. Gertrude wanted to comfort the women who seemed really upset, but she had no idea how to. *Sure do wish Pastor were here. He'd know what to say.* This thought made her feel guilty for skipping church so often. *Get me home, God, and I'll go to church Sunday. Promise.*

Samantha led the way to the small house, and Gertrude brought up the rear. When she stepped inside, it took a few seconds for her eyes to adjust to the indoor lighting of the cabin. Their host shut the door behind her, and she took a good look at him. He was a small but muscular man, dressed like a Mainer, in boots, blue jeans, and a plaid flannel shirt. Gertrude could make out the outline of a holster under his shirt. He caught her staring, and she tried to smile.

He nodded stoically.

"My name's Dave," he said, and she knew that it wasn't.

She nodded back. "We are much obliged for your help, Dave."

He smiled, as if they had just shared some secret, but she didn't know quite what it was. "Happy to help. But I'd be also be much obliged if, when this is over, you all forget you ever met me. I'm not really a people person."

Gertrude nodded. She took a step closer to him, and whispered, "Are you a spook?"

He chuckled dryly, and shook his head. "I'm not anything. I'm just a retired guy who likes to live in the woods. Like I said, not much of a people person. Why don't you make yourself comfortable. It could be quite a wait." Then he walked away, making it clear that their conversation was over.

No way he's old enough to be retired. Unless he's retired from the military. They can retire a lot younger, right? Gertrude surveyed the room. All the available seats were already taken. Samantha was sitting on the floor, her back against a wall, her eyes closed. Beside her stood an impressive gun cabinet, and it was chock-full of weapons. Beside that, another gun cabinet. More guns. She looked at "Dave." He was talking to Martha. There was definitely something weird about him, and yet, he wasn't giving her the heebie-jeebies at all.

At the other side of the cabin was a small kitchen. Beside that was a doorway, but a blanket hung in it, blocking her view of what lay beyond. Trying to act casually, she strolled along the wall, nodding to the women in her path, and eventually made it to the blanketed doorway. She reached out to move the blanket. She was only going to move it a bit. She only wanted a peek. But seemingly out of nowhere, Dave's hand covered hers. "I think there's plenty of room for all of us out here, don't you?"

She looked up at him.

He was smiling.

"I was just exploring," she said.

"I know."

"Could I trouble you for a glass of water?"

"Of course." He stepped back and used his right hand to make a sweeping invitation. He wanted her to walk toward the kitchenette, and he wasn't going to move until she did. So, grudgingly, she headed toward the sink, and he followed.

He rummaged in a cupboard until he found a glass. Then he held it under the faucet.

"Thanks, Dave," she said when he handed her the drink. "So, this place is awful neat and tidy for a man who lives alone."

"I understand you're the one who rescued all these women," Dave said.

Gertrude was aware that he was changing the subject, and that he was using flattery to do it. "I had some help," she said.

He nodded. "I wish I'd known something was going on up there. I saw that van go by frequently. At first, I just thought that woman was someone like me, someone who liked living in the woods, but I did get a little suspicious when she drove by so *often*. People who like to live in the woods usually stay in the woods. Anyway, I should've checked it out. I'm sorry that I didn't."

Gertrude nodded. "You strike me as a man who doesn't like to get involved."

Dave smirked. "Nice try, but really, Gertrude, there is no mystery to be solved here. I'm not a fugitive. I'm not a spy. I'm not anything. I'm just a guy in the woods."

"What's your last name?"

Dave began to show signs of exasperation. "Don't you want to drink your water?"

Gertrude took a small sip. "Could I use your phone?"

Dave looked at her, seeming to think about that. Then, apparently, he decided against it. "I've already called the police. They should be here any second. I'm sure they'll take you to a phone." He leaned back against his counter, crossed his arms, and looked out a window facing the road.

Gertrude drank her water.

16

When Gertrude woke up, she was lying on the floor, with no idea how she'd gotten there. A paramedic was asking her if she was OK. She looked around for Dave, and saw him standing near his front door, looking at her, smiling. She glared at him. *He drugged me!*

She looked at the paramedic, "He drugged me!"

"It's OK. You're OK. My name is Ashley, and we're going to get you to a hospital."

Gertrude sat up, which brought on an unpleasant bout of dizziness. She put her hand to her head. She looked around the room, and it looked like all the other women were still there. Another paramedic was tending to Dorothy. A police officer was talking to Samantha, and someone in a different uniform was standing beside Dave. She squinted at the patch on his shirt and decided he must be a game warden.

"No," Gertrude said, "you should get these other women to the hospital first. I'm fit as a fiddle."

Ashley smiled. "Do you need a stretcher, or can I help you walk to the ambulance?"

Gertrude looked at her. "I said, I don't want to go to the hospital. Take someone else."

The paramedic sighed and looked toward the cop, "Jack, can you help me get her into the ambulance?"

Jack flipped his notebook shut and strode across the room to Gertrude. He bent over and put her left arm around the back of his neck. "Up we go," he said, and in one smooth movement, pulled her to her feet. The paramedic held onto her right arm, and in this way, they escorted her out the door and to the ambulance. "Step right up," the officer said, and Gertrude stepped.

Ashley thanked Jack, and Jack vanished.

"Are you comfortable sitting, or would you rather lie down?" Ashley asked.

"Why don't you care that that man drugged me?"

"He said you fell asleep."

"I didn't just *fall asleep*."

Ashley looked at Gertrude. "I'm telling you, you *did*. Now let it go. You are safe. You are a hero. Leave it at that." She spoke into her radio. "Antoine, I'm going to stay out here with the patient. Can you get the others out?"

"Sure can, Ash."

Gertrude looked out the back of the ambulance to see the cabin door open. Three women, one of them Samantha, followed Jack to the police cruiser. He opened the door for them, and they climbed inside. Three others followed the game warden to the truck. And Antoine led three women toward the ambulance.

"Gonna be snug," Gertrude remarked.

"Yep, but we've done it before."

"Has someone already gone to help Sue?" Gertrude asked.

"Sue?"

"The kidnapper?"

"Oh! Yes. I haven't heard yet that they've found her, but yes, they're looking."

"We left her tied up," Gertrude said, suddenly feeling a little guilty about that.

Ashley patted Gertrude on the knee. "You did good, Gertrude. Real good." Then Ashley hopped out of the ambulance so that she could help the others climb in. Two slid onto the bench seat beside Gertrude. Ruth took Ashley's seat.

When they were all loaded, Ashley started to shut the back door of the bus. Gertrude looked out past her, and saw Dave standing in the doorway of his cabin. He smiled at Gertrude. And then waved.

17

At the Greenville Hospital, a kind woman in green scrubs asked Gertrude if she could call anyone for her. Gertrude didn't answer immediately. Normally, in circumstances such as these, she would call someone from her church, but this time she kind of wanted to call Calvin. But she didn't want to annoy him. And she wasn't sure he would even drive all the way to Greenville just to pick her up. As she chewed on her lip, trying to make a decision, Calvin appeared in the doorway. She felt her own face light up, and then tried to hide her joy. "Would you give me a ride home, Calvin?"

Calvin nodded.

Gertrude looked at the woman with the clipboard. "I'm all set. Thanks."

The woman left, and Calvin crossed the room to Gertrude. "Gertrude," he said, "you're famous."

She cackled. "What?"

"You're all over the news. Gertrude, Gumshoe saves lives. You're a hero. For real this time." He sat down in a chair beside her.

"Well, that's all well and good, but I really need my walker, and I miss my cats, and I think they must be starving—"

"I fed your cats."

"You what?"

"This morning. Before I heard the news. I knew you weren't home, so I fed your cats."

"Wowsa ... thanks, Calvin. I didn't know you had it in ya."

He chuckled. "Well, I don't. I really don't like cats. Or any other creatures that defecate indoors. So don't make a habit of getting yourself kidnapped."

She laughed too, but it was humorless. "I didn't do it on purpose, Calvin. I had this whole plan. But, well, she attacked me. She was crazy. Speaking of which, did they find her? Is she all right?"

Calvin raised an eyebrow. "You're worried about her? Little bit of Stockholm syndrome?"

"I don't know what that means, but yes, I'm a little worried about her. She was just a lonely, weird women who wanted friends. She didn't go about it in the best way, but I still don't want her to die in the forest, tied up in Virginia creeper."

Calvin barked with laughter. "You tied her up in Virginia creeper?"

"Well, I'm no plant expert, but it was some kind of creeper. 'Bout near ripped my hands open trying to pull it out of the ground."

Calvin smiled. "Well, yes, to answer your question, she is fine. She's right here in this very hospital, surrounded by State Troopers."

"And all the women? They're all right too?"

"Yes. Some of them definitely needed medical care. I heard that some of them hadn't been able to take their medications, but it sounds like they're all going to be OK."

"Sad, isn't it?" Gertrude mused.

"Which part?"

"All those women, just taken, taken out of their cars, out of their lives, and no one even missed them. Where were their families? Their friends? Their churches? How could someone be *stolen* and no one even notice it? If Sue hadn't slipped up and taken a young'un, we still wouldn't even know anything was wrong."

Calvin paused. "Yes. It's sad. But it's also over. Are you all set to go home?"

"Yes. The cops have already grilled me. They say I'm free to go."

"OK then, let's get you back to your feline entourage."

As they walked toward the door, Calvin asked, "What's it like, moving around without your walker?"

"Worse than snow in August."

Calvin chuckled, and held the hospital door open for Gertrude. The few people in the lobby stared at them as they left. "But I guess this means that you don't really need it, right?"

"This doesn't mean anything," Gertrude said. "I can go a few days without cheese too—doesn't mean I can live without it."

Calvin laughed. "You are certainly one of a kind, Gertrude." He opened the Cadillac door for her. "If someone stole you, all kinds of people would notice."

She smiled up at him. "Thanks, Calvin."

"You bet," he said, and shut her door.

When he had settled into his own seat, she asked, "Have you talked to Hale?"

"Yes, why?"

"Just wondering if he was mad at me."

"Oh, I think so. I think that's sort of a constant state of mind for him. I called him as soon as I realized you were missing."

"How'd you know I was missing?"

"When I found your walker without you in it. And your cell phone was ground into the mud in your yard. I think you're going to need a new one of those, by the way. Anyway, he flew into action. That's when you were first on the news, as a missing person at eleven o'clock. And by the five o'clock news today, you were a statewide hero. You might actually get some paying clients now, which terrifies me."

"Speaking of paying clients—"

"Yes, I talked to Andy too. He showed up at my place at midnight last night. I wasn't too happy about that, but he made up for it when he called me today. That's how I knew where you were. Samantha called him, and he called me. One big happy family."

"I see," Gertrude said thoughtfully.

"What is it?"

"What is what?"

"I don't know. You're being pensive."

"Well, I was just thinking. I need your help with something. But I don't really want to hear your commentary about it."

Calvin groaned. "What is it now?"

"I think it's time for me to get a driver's license."

18

Gertrude slept for thirteen hours straight.

She awoke to someone knocking on her door. She sat up, knocking a few cats off her in the process, and slid her feet into her slippers. Her hair looked like she had rubbed a can of mousse in it and then stood between opposing high-powered fans, but she didn't think to smooth it down. She wanted to see who was at the door.

There had been a few reporters there the night before, but she had given them a statement, and they had happily trotted along.

She peeked out a window and saw Andy and Samantha on her steps.

She opened the door. Andy jumped at the sight of her. Samantha elbowed him in the side.

"Morning!" Gertrude said brightly.

"Morning," Andy said. There was an awkward pause while they both stared at her hair. Then Andy asked, "Could we come in for a minute?"

"Oh!" Gertrude said, stepping backward, and sweeping her hand in a 'come on in' gesture. "Of course! Mi casa is you casa!"

They stepped inside. She closed the door behind them, and Andy handed her an envelope. "Here's what I have right now, and I'm sure I owe you more, so just let me know what my balance is. I'll pay you as soon as I can."

Gertrude peeked into the envelope. It was full of twenties. She looked up at Andy. Then she handed him the envelope. "You know what? Don't worry about it. I was glad to help."

Andy's jaw dropped. "But, Gertrude—"

"No, really, it's all right. If you were rolling in the clams"—Andy frowned in confusion—

"that'd be one thing. But I know you're not. So really, this one's on the house."

"Wow, Gertrude, I don't know how we will ever thank you. And I mean, I was thinking that *before* you just handed me this envelope." Andy took a deep breath. "I gotta admit, I thought I was nuts hiring you. But I wasn't. You did it. I don't know how, but you really did it. You saved my Samantha." He looked at Samantha then, his eyes full of adoration. He pulled her to him, and kissed her on the top of the head.

"All right, you lovebirds get out of here now. And Andy, you should know, I couldn't have done it without Samantha. Well, actually, that's not true. I could have done it without Samantha. But still, you should know that she was a big help."

Andy smiled at Gertrude, then at Samantha again. Gertrude hadn't known Andy could smile that much. She opened the door for them and shooed them outside. Then she headed toward the bathroom for a visit that was rapidly becoming overdue. She'd only taken about three steps when there was another knock at the door. She sighed and turned back toward it. As she opened it, she loudly said, "I told you, don't worry about—"

Deputy Hale was standing on her steps.

"Oh, you."

He smirked.

"What can I do for you, Hale? Come for some investigative tips?"

He shook his head, his smirk fading. "Gertrude, I don't know how you did what you did. Sounds to me like you were reckless and got blind lucky. But I also don't care. You want to get yourself killed, go ahead. I obviously can't stop you. But that's not why I'm here."

"Oh no? You selling Girl Scout cookies?"

"I know you think you're funny. But you're really not. I am here because there's been a complaint against you."

"What? From who? Sue? Dave?"

"Who's Dave? You know what, never mind. No, from Colby Rodin. He's a PI in town—"

"I know who he is."

"And he's saying that you're operating without a license. Wants me to put a stop to it."

"And you're his errand boy?"

Hale frowned. "No, but we do work closely with him sometimes, and I would like to stay on good professional terms. The thing is, he has a point—"

"I never told anyone I was a private investigator."

"No, but you told them you were a gumshoe."

"And is there a law against that?"

"Gertrude, I'm just saying, you're treading on thin ice here. If something were to happen, you could easily get sued."

Gertrude cackled. "It's hard to get blood out of a turnip!"

Hale sighed. He rubbed his forehead. "I'm just saying. I think your choices are, find another hobby, or, and it pains me to say this, get licensed."

Gertrude's eyes grew wide. "Get licensed? Don't you need to go to school for that?"

Hale nodded.

"All right. I'll think about it. Is that all?"

Hale nodded again. "I think your heart's in the right place, Gertrude. You helped to rescue those women, but you could have just called me when you figured out who it was—"

"And would you have listened to me?"

Hale gave her a long look. "How about this, Gertrude. I really, really hope there isn't a next time, but if there is, I promise to listen to you."

19

After a big lunch of saltines, seriously sharp cheddar, and pickles, Gertrude headed over to Calvin's.

"Can you take me to the Bureau of Motor Vehicles and AmeriCell?" she asked when he opened the door. "I need a driver's license and a new jitterbug."

"Isn't this usually stuff you call the CAP bus for?" he said, turning toward his living room and walking away from her, leaving the door open.

She stepped inside and shut it behind her. "Yes, but I don't want to take the CAP bus to the BMV."

"Why not?"

Because, what if I fail? Everyone will know. "Because I just don't. Now are you going to take me or not?"

"I'll take you to AmeriCell, but you don't need to go to the BMV. You can do it all online. I've already printed out the application. It's on the desk."

Gertrude hobbled over to the desk.

"How's your back?" he asked.

"Much better now. Thank you."

"Probably all that walking around without your walker."

She gave the back of his head a dirty look, and then looked down at the application. "Ten dollars? Are they bonkers? Ten dollars just to apply?"

Calvin guffawed. "You just wait. Driving is expensive. Besides, isn't that Andy fella going to pay you?"

"OK, I'll fill this out," she said, avoiding his question. She sat down and started to write. It didn't take long. "Do you have an envelope?"

"Top of desk."

"And a stamp?"

"Good grief, Gertrude. Can't you do anything for yourself?" He got up and walked over to the desk. He opened a drawer and pulled out a stamp.

"Also, can you write a check for ten dollars? I don't have a checkbook. I'll pay you back."

"If it means I no longer have to drive you around everywhere."

"I'm getting a driver's license, Calvin. I still don't have a car. You going to let me drive the Cadillac?"

"When pigs fly."

"Danno lets McGarrett drive his car."

Calvin smirked. "You are no McGarrett, and Danno doesn't *let* McGarrett drive. McGarrett just does." He ripped a check from his checkbook. "Not that I'm suggesting you try to do the same. Come on. Let's go."

"Where?"

"The post office. And AmeriCell."

Gertrude expected, when she got her new phone, that there would be a pile of voicemails waiting for her. She was wrong. "Huh," she said. "Didn't you think this case would bring me more customers? I mean, with the publicity and all?" She looked at Calvin.

"Can you lean back, please?" He was trying to pull out of the AmeriCell parking lot. "I can't see anything but your hair." He pulled out into traffic. "It's only been a day. I wouldn't worry about it, Gert. Cases seem to find you. And while you've certainly gotten some press, it's still a small town. Not much crime. Small state. Not much crime."

"It didn't feel like a small state when we were driving on endless dirt roads."

"True. Big state by land. Small state by people."

"Which reminds me," Gertrude said. "You wanna go for a ride?"

"No."

"Remember how I told you about Dave? Let's go pay him a visit. Maybe he'll tell us who he is, if there's not so many people around."

Calvin looked at her. "You want me to drive three hours into the woods to visit a man with lots of guns who specifically asked to never see you again?"

Gertrude nodded. "Yes."

"Sorry. Not happening. And don't threaten to hitchhike this time. We both know you'd never get picked up on those roads. Except maybe by a moose."

"What if he's a *really bad* guy? Don't you want to figure out why he's hiding in the woods?"

"Gertrude, he helped you ladies. And some people just like their privacy. I used to like my privacy, back when I had some."

"Calvin, he *drugged* me!"

"Or you just fell asleep."

"You didn't see the way he smiled at me."

"Yeah, let's slap the cuffs on him. The man smiled. So, so suspicious!"

"All right. Can you drop me off at Samantha's apartment then?"

"You've got to be kidding me."

"What?"

"You're going to make that sweet girl drive you into the bowels of Aroostook County?"

"She owes me."

"Fine. Just fine. I'll take you. But you're going to be quiet the whole way. Deal?"

20

Calvin needn't have worried. Gertrude slept the entire drive north. He poked her a few times to ask for directions, but then she would drift off to sleep again. It was starting to get dark out when he gave her arm a good shake.

"What? Where—"

"Stay awake. I think we're close."

She rubbed her eyes and cracked the window.

"I've got the air conditioning on," Calvin said.

"Need a bit of fresh air to wake me up."

"And I need you to stop ruining my gas mileage. Now roll the window up."

She rolled her eyes, and the window up.

"There!" she cried.

"What?"

"Right there! Up ahead, on the right."

He slowed down.

"You don't need to slow down yet."

He ignored her, and crept up to the driveway. "There's no mailbox."

"I don't think he gets much mail." Gertrude looked around. "His truck's not here. I don't have a good feeling about this."

"Me neither. I wish we'd gotten here before dusk. Or even better, not come at all."

Gertrude got out of the car and then wrestled her walker out of the back.

Calvin climbed out too, grumbling the whole time. "I can't believe I let you talk me into this. Now I've got to drive home, a hundred miles, dirt roads, probably hit a moose and die …"

Gertrude knocked on the door. There was no answer. She knocked again. Nothing. The knob turned easily in her hand. She pushed the door open.

"Gertrude!" Calvin tried.

Gertrude went inside. Her fingers found a light switch, and she flicked it, but nothing happened. Her stomach sank. All the furniture in the room was still there, but the room still looked emptier somehow. Gertrude looked to her left. The gun cabinets were empty. She saw a piece of paper on the table. She went to it. It read:

> Gertrude, I assure you, I am not a criminal, and I beg you to not try to find me. I was happy to help you ladies, but now I really just want to be left alone. — Dave

"Well, I'll be darned," Calvin said, reading over her shoulder. "He knew you were coming."

Gertrude looked around the now-empty cabin. "That rascal. I wonder where he went."

Calvin put his hand on her shoulder. "Let's go, Gertrude. We're not going to find him.

Let's get you home. We should start studying for your driver's test."

"Can I practice driving on the way home? It's all dirt roads! No traffic!"

Calvin laughed all the way to the car.

Large Print Books by Robin Merrill

Gertrude, Gumshoe Cozy Mystery Series
Introducing Gertrude, Gumshoe
Gertrude, Gumshoe: Murder at Goodwill
Gertrude, Gumshoe and the VardSale Villain
Gertrude, Gumshoe: Slam Is Murder
Gertrude, Gumshoe: Gunslinger City
Gertrude, Gumshoe and the Clearwater Curse

Wing and a Prayer Mysteries
The Whistle Blower
The Showstopper
The Pinch Runner

Shelter Trilogy (featuring Gertrude)
Shelter
Daniel
Revival

Piercehaven Trilogy
Piercehaven
Windmills
Trespass

Standalone Novella
Grace Space (the original Gertrude story)

Robin Merrill also writes sweet romance as
Penelope Spark:
The Billionaire's Cure
The Billionaire's Secret Shoes
The Billionaire's Blizzard
The Billionaire's Chauffeuress
The Billionaire's Christmas

Want the inside scoop?
Visit robinmerrill.com to join
Robin's Readers!

Made in the USA
Middletown, DE
19 August 2020